Home from England

Home from England

JAMES RYAN

Phoenix House
LONDON

First published in Great Britain in
1995 by Phoenix House
Orion House
5 Upper St Martin's Lane
London WC2H 9EA

A CIP catalogue record is available
from the British Library

ISBN: 1 897 580 72X (cased)
ISBN: 1 897 580 673 (paperback)

Typeset by Selwood Systems, Midsomer Norton

Printed in Great Britain by Butler & Tanner Ltd,
Frome and London

part one

I

A big tree stands right in the middle of the green, but only the top of it can be seen from the far side of the moor. That's where we're meeting to plan the final stage of our mission: Operation Balooba.

It is August and humid, just like the Congo.

We had spent most of the morning fighting our way through the tangling briars and were, at last, getting near the river. Down below in the shelter of its high brown clay bank we knew we could make headway without being seen.

The shallow water is warm in places. My feet brush against the feelers dangling from the iris roots, all white and limp. The river bed is covered in soft spongy algae, loaches and minnows dart into it, fleeing for cover.

Far away through the undergrowth, I can see part of the stone wall above which the great bulk of the tree towers into the sky. In its shade the houses curl in on themselves, huddling, their backs hunched up.

'If we're captured, they'll strap a metal bowl to your stomach. There'll be a rat inside – hungry and starving. Your hands'll be tied. See. And the rat will eat through you starting with your skin.'

At the base of the wall the river turns, swooches round and lunges headlong towards the mill race.

'Right. Ready, everyone ready for combat?'

'Charge.'

I'm first over the wall and I race towards the tree, throw myself against it and look over my shoulder. My face tightens. The bark of the tree smells like stale biscuits. One by one the others join me. We storm across the green, faces wild, and make for the lane behind the houses.

In the distance, the old men sit watching.

Down at the end of this lane there is a dump. Someone has set fire to a big stripey horsehair mattress. It's awkwardly bunched on top of all the straggling garbage, smouldering, one line of silvery smoke going straight up into the air. In the centre of this mattress there is a red and orange blood stain.

We try to create flames by blowing and blowing and blowing. The scorching smell makes me cough and my eyes fill with pain.

Ding Mackey says someone had a baby on the mattress. His brother, Shem, jeers at him, telling us that Ding doesn't know what he is talking about. Then they glare at each other with their eyes all squinched up. This is what they always do before they fight and they spend a lot of time fighting, all day, somedays. I stand beside Hegarty as Shem strikes out – trying to tear Ding's face by pushing some of his fingers into his mouth. Nobody ever stops them because we all know that the two of them would turn on anyone who tried. Shem grips Ding's hair and drags him up the lane and back onto the green.

The old men, glassy-eyed and silent, peer as if through mist

4

while the Mackeys pass right in front of them, shouting and screaming at each other.

The back door of our house is open and from the bottom of the garden I can see my father's gaberdine coat draped over the gas cylinder. But even if that coat wasn't there I would still have known he was inside because there is always something different about the house when he is home.

He has been here for a week, exactly half his holidays. He comes every August, home from England where he works. I don't know when he first went there, not exactly anyhow. I think it was sometime during the winter after I was born. 1951. He was forty-three and at the time he thought he was going only for a few months. So did my mother. It wasn't a big plan to change everything. They don't make that kind of plan. With them, it's more day to day, and that's probably the way it was then.

His visits are all more or less the same. The days are spent eating and going for short walks. Always the same walk, as if he had lost something and had to go over his journey again and again, searching. Sometimes I go with him, glad to be there when people see he has come home. He says hello to everyone but it ends there, even though he sometimes slows down a little and looks at people for an instant longer than they look at him.

The year before last when he was home, I got the notion that he had done something wrong, or something peculiar, something that made people keep away. In an out-of-the-blue moment, surprising even myself, I asked Bríd about this. Bríd is my mother but we have never called her any of the usual mother names. We call her what my grandmother always called her. Bríd. My grandmother was the boss in our house right up until the minute she died last year. When I asked Bríd if he had done something wrong she swung round, impatient and cross, and asked me what sort of person I was. But as soon as she said it her face softened.

5

'Some people just don't remember him straight away, that's all,' she said.

I believed her but I went on wondering how he could be so interested in people who didn't seem all that interested in him. And I still wonder about it.

Our window darkens as one of the old men passes on his way to the low stumpy wall at the bottom of the green where they always sit. Some of the others are there already, settling in for the afternoon, nodding across the green to the middle distance.

When I see that the Mackeys, Canice Hegarty and Lynch are sitting on the embankment opposite our house, waiting for me, I stand up to leave. On my way out I tell Bríd that I am going to the castle. She looks over towards my father.

'You better ask your father. He knows how dangerous it is.'

My father says that the castle is very dangerous.

I wait at the door for a few seconds thinking that there is more to follow but there isn't so I leave. Then I wait outside, listening, expecting them to talk about me but they say nothing.

The tar at the edge of the road melts in the balmy August heat. Hegarty and Lynch poke it with sticks, jostling and bolting like colts as they try to smear each other, laughing all the while, shouting and looking at us to see if we are laughing too.

The castle stands in the middle of an open field. Any proper path over to it has long since turned back to pasture land. On our way over we watch cattle file into the castle, defeated by the heat and the mechanical buzz of the flies which pester them all the time. Inside, with their hooves deep in dung, they stand flicking their tails.

'We'll trap them inside.'

Right away I know I should not have said that. I should have waited until I had a plan and then said something like,

6

'I have an idea,' real quick, 'I have an idea.' But it's too late. The others are already running towards the castle and when I get there Hegarty is in charge, telling them what to do in a loud voice. They place an old sheet of galvanized iron across the entrance and pile stones up behind it to hold it in place.

We climb the outside wall of the castle, to the place where the stones have fallen away making a jagged, cave-like opening more than thirty feet from the ground. The climb is tricky. Talking stops until, one by one, we edge our way up and into what was once a large square room. But it has no ceiling now and most of the floor has fallen through. By staying close to the wall it is just about possible to go the whole way round.

Down below the cattle shuffle and grunt. One of them mounts the one in front in a half-hearted way. As the noise fills out above them, they begin to get uneasy and stumble against each other. Hegarty, still acting as though he is in charge, starts shouting. Then the Mackeys hiss and roar.

One of the cattle rears against the blockade at the doorway, getting its front legs up onto the pile of stones outside. It pounds forward in jerky leaps, frantic, its eyes rolling backwards until the pupils disappear.

Hegarty showers it with rocks and mortar, driving it into such a panic that it breaks through. Within minutes the rest of the cattle stumble over the mangled sheet of galvanized iron and the rocks.

Hegarty leans out to throw a final stone.

The pace at which he falls forward is slow and measured and for that moment I feel no sense of alarm.

It is not me.

It is Hegarty. And his twisting movements do not look like the movements of a person. But his scream, charged with terror and broken by hoarse changes in pitch, forces me to look at what is happening. I try to resist, struggling to move backwards in time and hold on to the world as it had been that split second before he fell. I spread my hands, press them against the cold and damp of the wall. But everything I see and hear as I move back becomes a powerful omen of all that has already happened. And I stand, like the others, mute and quaking, moving forward, moving back and then forward again as Hegarty raises himself to a kneeling position.

We watch every move he makes, every twitch.

And we don't speak. Not a word, even when we know that there is nothing wrong and that he is unhurt.

Hegarty looks down at his clothes, crying and gulping breath in between sobs. He tries to stop, but he can't. When he sees that we are all staring at him he shouts 'fuck' and he repeats it so many times that we start laughing. Hegarty laughs too and for a while it seems as if it is all over, but soon he is crying again. When he stands up he turns and we see that one side of his face is totally covered in dung.

We all point at him, laughing in an exaggerated way until he looks up at the Mackeys and then directly at me, drawing his lips together in a concentrated effort to stop crying.

'If you don't shut your mouth laughing, I'll break it for you.'

I try to stop.

'Did you hear me, did you, did ... ' his voice chokes up.

I look around, hoping that Lynch or one of the Mackeys will say something to him but they just look at me, making sure I know that I'm the one who is being threatened.

'Did you hear what I said?' Hegarty roars, this time in a clear voice.

From the safety of my perch thirty feet above him I shout back.

'I heard you alright Hegarty and if you weren't covered in cowshite I'd push your face in.'

The others start laughing again but this time their laughter is dry and broken in the way that put-on laughter often is. Then when one of Hegarty's shoes gets stuck in the dung the laughter gets shaky, slowly trailing into a singsong chant. In his struggle to get his shoe out he falls forward, looks back at the shoe buried in the dung and decides to leave it there. When he finally gets to the doorway he reaches out to remove the crumpled sheet of galvanized iron but pulls his hand back as if it had been burned. The top of the galvanized iron sheet is covered in blood and all along the jagged edge there are tufts of cattle hair and bits of white fatty flesh.

Hegarty looks around and back up towards us. Then, gathering all his anger into one fierce expression, he fixes on me.

'It's just as well for you that you won't be living around here much longer.'

The others are quiet. They glance sideways at me, waiting for my answer.

'Who are you talking about Hegarty?'

'You – I'm talking about you. Shook you, didn't it.'

All around the clouds have fallen to form a sort of dome and against this metallic sky the world looks stark. At the far side of the castle hundreds of crows are circling the beech trees, clamouring hoarsely about a storm that has already broken.

Hegarty sits down. He is shivering and just about to cry again when he leaps to his feet, rushes back into the castle and without saying a word to any of us, or even looking up at us, lifts his shoe from the dung, turns and jumps over the remains of the barricade.

There is a smell of sulphur as the rain cools the air. Hegarty stretches out his arms as if he wants to get wet on purpose and after a minute or two, when he is totally sodden, he sets off at an even gallop towards the road back home.

We stand in under a narrow ledge waiting for the rain to ease, telling each other about all the different ways defenders of the castle could kill and maim their attackers. But soon we stop talking, aware that the day has ended. When days end

9

like this, and sometimes even years and maybe decades too, people sense that nothing can change the way things have turned out. Things end by themselves and there is a sort of in-between feeling waiting for them to end officially. That's how it is as we watch the white rain pound and hack the castle field. Hegarty, barely visible in the distance, scampers off, like one of those dwarfs from the olden days who has just told a riddle.

By the time I get home tea is well over. I begin to explain why I am so late – Hegarty's fall and the rain – but I haven't got very far when my father cuts in to tell me how worried Bríd was and then he tells me to go straight up to bed.

Bríd is standing beside him and I know by looking at her that this is all her idea. Sometimes she even tells him what to say to me, when I'm standing there waiting for it to be said. But she always or nearly always adds something like 'go on do what you're told' or 'do what your father tells you'. This time she just says nothing.

Looking out my bedroom window and down on to the green I think about what happened in the castle. No matter how much I go over it all I cannot come to the end of thinking about it. I think of Hegarty and how he is nearly two years older then me and how, until about a month ago, just before the school holidays, he used to keep telling me what to do. Then there was a fight, not just a scrap, a long drawn out fight and although he says that he won, it is obvious from the way he says it that he didn't. I am thinking about the end of that fight when my bedroom door opens and Bríd walks in carrying a plate and a cup. I look at the sandwich which she leaves on the window sill beside me.

'It's sardine.' As she speaks she starts picking things up off the floor.

'We aren't going to England to live are we?'

'Who said that?'

'No one.'

I think of Hegarty running across the castle field and then the crows rising up from the beech trees.

'It's not decided yet. Now eat up your supper.'

'When will it be decided?'

'Not for the time being, give me that cup and I'll get you some milk.'

Once I'd asked the question I did not want Bríd to answer because I knew by the way it had emerged, as if of its own accord, and the way so much fell into place, that no matter what else she said we were definitely going.

She went downstairs to get the milk but she didn't come back.

2

After tea on the evening before he goes back, my father leaves
the house for his usual walk. I follow him out, quickstepping
along. A whole week has passed without any talk of England.
I keep waiting for him to say something, afraid to mention it
myself in case he gets the idea that I'm keen to go. He slows
down a little as we get near the place where the old men sit.
Moratorium Row is what it's called because during the war
for independence two or maybe three of them were on the
Black and Tan death list.

They all draw breath loudly and brace themselves, pre-
paring to speak.

'Great day.'

'Great day,' one of them replies.

The next one says 'great day' too.

'Aye.'

'That's the way.'

We move on, but we haven't gone very far when my father

slows down to take stock of the two cars parked outside the church at the top of the green. A third arrives as he stands looking.

I can see the hope settle on his face just before the words 'it's a funeral' slip quietly from the side of his mouth. Slowly he turns to ask the old men who has died. They answer psalm-like, all in line as though they have been practising before we arrived.

'Padge Delaney of Coolfaddin.'

'Been in the hospital this twelve months.'

'Got a stroke.'

'Coming to the church this evening, burial tomorrow morning.'

'Never sick a day in his life.'

'He'll be here in a minute.'

We stand waiting for the hearse to arrive, glad to be stopping there at Moratorium Row because we are not very far from the corner where my father's pace usually loses its sense of purpose.

The hearse arrives and slows down to a walking pace. The church bell peals out across the green and the women come out of the houses. The old men ease themselves off the wall and one by one slide into the funeral procession, like slugs. They tell each other about the dead man, saying all the things they always say, who he is related to, what he did in the fight for freedom, all that sort of thing. My father listens and then passes on the information, all about how the dead man stayed at home on the night of the big fire all those years ago. Then my father explains that the coffin is only coming to our church because the dead man's wife inherited a plot in the cemetery, adding 'that's where she'll be buried herself'. A stalky-looking man beside us, listening with his left ear pushed into my father's face, repeats the last bit, 'that's where she'll be buried', then bolts away and in a very stern way, adds 'with her own I suppose'. The three of us look around and into the car where she is sitting between her relations. Her eyes are all red and her mouth is a little open.

I love the inside of the church. It is full of importance. Even the one lost glove lying on the high sill above where I am kneeling has a sort of sacredness about it. After the prayers we stand about outside and several people nod and smile in our direction. My father is more than pleased with it all and when we get home he starts naming the people we saw at the church. He asks Bríd lots of questions about them and others, people who live miles away, people I didn't think he knew. She gives yes and no answers in a pleasant way, all the time moving about the room picking things up and folding clothes. Then he asks a question about the family who used to live up beyond the church, the Farrells. After a very long time Bríd says she is not sure and the conversation trickles to a close. I want to say England, but I can't. During the silence that follows I look out the kitchen window and across the green at the light spindling out from the big tree, drawing in the day.

After a little while Bríd goes over some of the names mentioned earlier, fixing on questions my father had asked her, adding bits of information here and there, edging us back calmly to by-the-way talk about people.

Agnes and Gretta, my sisters, are playing under the table. Bríd calls Gretta and they both creep out, complaining about having to sleep in my room when my father is home on holiday. Bríd tells them to stop but they just go on whining.

Maybe I should have said England. In bed I say it lots of times slowly, then real fast, then in an exaggerated way, moving my mouth around as if it was a very difficult word to pronounce.

In the morning the light leaks through the gaps and crevices where the curtains join awkwardly. It is concentrated into thin luminous beams that stretch the whole way across the room and quiver on the door. Agnes and Gretta are playing out on the landing and down below them, sitting on the second last step of the stairs, my father is polishing his shoes for the funeral. Without turning around he moves to let me pass, and as I squeeze by he tells me that I'd better hurry. He has his coat on, all ready to go.

During the week, we had gone to a match in the town. We were first to arrive. After a long time a man carrying a big bundle of jerseys came and my father spoke to him for a while but he went away again. Then we walked around the hurling field several times. We must have been there at least two hours before the match began and my father didn't think there was anything wrong with that.

It's the same now. He is sitting at the bottom of the stairs shining his shoes and the funeral Mass won't be starting for well over an hour. He waits at the door and then drifts down towards Moratorium Row, dawdles a bit there and then makes his way back up here again, all the time looking up towards the church to see if there is any sign of things getting under way.

The priest from the town has a grey Hillman estate and when it swerves around the corner at the bottom of the green everything swings into action. Bells ring. Doors open and close. More cars come. Small clusters of people gather and the whole thing builds and builds and my father and I are in the middle of it, marching up the green towards the church.

The priest stands with his back to the congregation. He is magnificently dressed. His outer layer, a great coat, is studded with silver sequins and embroidered with threads that glisten when he moves. His solemn chant echoes around the church and sunshine bursts through the diamonds of grainy glass, making everything flicker and jump. The servers move mechanically, standing and kneeling in unison, clanking bells and chirping responses. The coffin lies on a stand in the middle of the aisle, covered with Mass cards. Three tall candles burn on either side. When Mass is over these candles are removed so that the priest can circle the coffin with a smoking thurible. He lifts it and lets it fall to get rid of the last of the evil forces which until he died had invisibly tried to claim the man's soul. Then the priest turns around and with a milky face tells everybody that Padge Delaney has earned a place in paradise.

The coffin is hoisted up, carried out on to the gravel path and over towards the open grave. The old men are out in force, leaning against the graveyard wall, afraid to court death by moving too close.

They were soldiers once. Most of them fought in the First World War and all of them fought in the War of Independence. That is when they became heroes, almost fifty years ago, when they won freedom for Ireland. At the time everyone thought that when one era ends a new one begins. But it didn't turn out like that. It went on being the end of an era and the old men went on being heroes and everybody waited and waited and waiting became an era in itself.

The priest says 'from dust' and before he says 'to dust' he lifts the holy water sprinkler high into the air. With that the glinting shovel pan strikes the pile of clay and in very little time the grave is filled, stroked and patted.

The widow, her face inflamed with grief, is bundled away from the scene. My father and I follow behind.

'Well, you'll have the swimming pools and the cinemas and you'll be going to Battersea Funfair.'

As soon as he says 'well', I know that something about us all going to England is about to follow. It is as if we had been talking about it for days and he was reminding me of something he had said already.

All I manage to say is 'swimming pools' and I say it in such an unsure way that my father thinks I am asking a question and so replies immediately.

'Yes, in England, in England there are swimming pools.'

He looks at me sideways and I can feel my face drain of all

the interest I had gathered up to say 'swimming pools' for the second time. Then, he says 'self service shops', impatiently, and after a long interval 'motorways'. I repeat these words after him, aware that he is running out of things to say about England. He more or less admits this himself when he turns towards me and says 'anyway you'll have a great time'.

I fall behind and read the names written on the gravestones. Then I pick up some of the coloured stones covering the graves. When my father has moved a few steps ahead I follow. Sweat dribbles down the back of his neck on to the shiny black rim of his coat collar. He is bulky but his shadow is lean and long and moves without effort. All the time I'm thinking about England but everything I know about it seems separate from the thought that we are going to live there. I know that girls who are not married and are going to have babies have to go there. I know that we won our freedom from England. I have seen a film about it, *Mise Eire*, twice. The first time the whole school went by bus to the cinema in Thurles and then last year it was shown in school. All the windows were darkened and a big white screen sheet was hung from a hook up near the ceiling. It stretched the whole way down to the ground and it covered the altar at the top of the classroom.

Most of the people who come home from England on holidays dress in the latest styles. The couples hold hands as they saunter around the place and they have this air of knowing which makes England seem like a much better place than here or the town. But then some of them cry when they are getting into the hackney car to go to the station to catch the boat train.

Dinner on the day my father goes back is always different. It takes longer, like on Sundays. Twice during it, I have to go out to tell Hegarty and the others, who are waiting for me to go for a swim, that I won't be long.

The river bank is powdery dry and furrowed, large deep

cracks running all the way down to the water. Hegarty says there could be an earthquake if it gets any hotter. We laugh at him as we move inwards to where the water cools and darkens. I draw my breath and wade downstream. Hegarty stands on the river bank, fully clothed, watching the Mackeys trying to drown each other. He won't swim and won't say why.

From the moor I can see part of the road to the town. It curves down and then around toward the houses which, from here, waver in the dusty August heat, all exhausted into a sort of timelessness. And it all stays thin and distant, even though we are almost back at the stone wall where the old men sit, panting like dogs with their mouths hanging into the layers of skin lolling in hoops over their collars.

Across the green Hegarty's mother, Babs, walks up past the houses. She is on her way back from the convent in the town. She goes there every day and she stands waiting at the kitchen door of the convent until this nun with a very white face hands out a basin covered with a greyish coloured cloth. Then she carries it home as if it was something important. Other people who get food from the nuns in the town empty whatever they get into a jug or something – anything, even a jam jar. Then they put it back into the bag they brought it in and it's just like they had been to the shops. But Babs brings no jug or basin of her own and for the three mile walk back from the town she holds the convent basin way out in front of her. Bríd says that Babs wants everyone, especially her husband's sisters, to know that she has to beg.

Hegarty is ashamed of it all. He pretends not to notice his mother, who is holding the basin even further out in front of her than usual. Another thing that shows he is ashamed is the way he is always telling people that his father is coming home from England. But if anyone asks him when, he says something stupid like that's for me to know and you to find out. I have never seen his father but there is a photograph of him wedged into the corner of the gilt frame of the Sacred Heart picture in their house. The photograph is dark but the top of it has curled down and the pink glow of the Sacred Heart lamp lights up his face.

Babs stops at our gate. As she speaks she moves her head from side to side ducking and craning as if things were being thrown at her from behind. Bríd, who is polishing the door knocker, turns around, surprised. They look at each other blankly, then Babs speaks again.

'I said the place is a credit to you.'

Bríd smiles and is just about to say something when Babs speaks again.

'A credit to you.'

Bríd smiles again.

'Unnatural weather, I can't ever remember it being this hot.'

Babs looks down the green towards her own house, giving the impression that she is considering what Bríd had said about the weather. As she replies she glances over at me.

'It won't be long now, will it?'

Bríd ignores the question and goes on talking about the hot weather – but then, changing tone suddenly, and looking directly at me says,

'The end of September probably.'

Hegarty, who until then was standing right beside me, slowly edges over towards Babs, squinting and grimacing as though he was meeting me for the first time. Then he and his mother back away. As they move she starts naming people we all know who went to England, listing all the things they now own and all the ways things have got better for them. I stand there wishing that Hegarty had been killed when he fell in the castle. I try to imagine him lying there dead but instead my ears fill with the sound of the crows rising up from the beech trees. When they are gone I know Bríd will probably start pretending that nothing about us going to England is definite yet. I drift away slowly, trying to let on that I had not really been following the conversation. Then once I'm over on the green and in the shade of the big tree I walk more quickly, heading down towards Moratorium Row.

Babs and Hegarty move further and further away from Bríd. All the time Babs goes on telling her, in a loud voice, about things we will be getting when we go to England. The old men look across, peering as they try to figure out what's going on. Eventually they turn back to each other, muttering their own explanation.

'Must be the heat.'

'Must be,' one of them replies.

'The heat,' another one adds.

A minute or so later Fran Dooley looks over towards Babs and Hegarty. He is very soft-spoken in a worn-out sort of way. But in bygone days, those days when they all fought for independence and freedom, he was more fierce than the fiercest. The spongy mallow textured bags under his eyes pucker before he speaks.

'Must be the heat alright.'

Some of them make low sounds of agreement and as these sounds die away the whole place seems to wobble for a moment as though it could move back in time just as easily as it moves forward.

After a while our door opens. Bríd and my father stand there, each waiting for the other to walk to the gate first.

'I'll slip up to Queenie's while I have the chance – before I start getting the tea. I'd hate her to hear it from strangers.'

My father says 'aye' and walks down towards Moratorium Row.

Queenie is my aunt, Bríd's sister – her only sister. She lives up beyond the church. I decide to go there with Bríd, thinking that she will tell Queenie everything about us going to England.

Queenie must have seen us when we passed the window because she opens the door just as Bríd is about to knock.

Wearing a large blue and white apron with ruffles sticking out like wings, she beckons us to come in. Then dashes back in, touching various things in a particular way before moving backwards to touch them in a different way.

My mother speaks before we get into the kitchen.

'We're going, it's definite – as soon as Dan gets a place for us.'

'I see,' and there is a long pause before Queenie continues. 'When will he be getting the place?'

'When he goes back.'

Queenie says nothing but she bustles about which makes it seem as if she hasn't got the time to think about what Bríd is telling her.

'Well, after he goes back,' Bríd begins to tell it all again, 'after he goes back. He's catching the boat train this evening. Next week he'll start looking, so it should be the end of September, probably.'

Queenie faces the cooker. She is moving the pots and pans around and then moving them back to where they were in the first place. She asks Bríd to look out the window to see if Michael is coming. Her voice is tight as if she had to give instructions at some sort of emergency like a car crash.

'No sign yet.'

'Would you fold his paper and put it beside his plate.'

Queenie gives more instructions and after a few minutes they are both carrying on as if nothing at all had been said about us going to England. Bríd refolds the paper and Queenie straightens the knife to make it parallel to the fork. Then they both look towards the window as it darkens – Michael, wheeling his bike – Michael moving like a figure on a merry-go-round. 'It's Michael,' Queenie whispers and her pace quickens. We move towards the door, saying goodbye in the way we always say goodbye.

Outside, as we pass the window, I see Queenie. She is even busier now. She lifts a saucepan full of potatoes to the sink to drain the water. Her elbows jut out in every direction. The steam rises and clouds around her face which is all twisted. Her mouth moves downwards as she mumbles something to herself. When I see that she is crying I look away.

We walk past the church and down towards the green. Sunlight shoots through the tree making pools of light on the footpath. I step into the light and jump across the shaded areas. I swerve at a sharp angle, brushing past Bríd who smiles and says that in the end it will all be for the best. I say nothing because I do not want what she has said to change.

When my father comes in she tries to talk about what it will be like when we are all living in England. Every time he answers one of her questions he stands up and walks over to the window, looks out for a few seconds and then walks back slowly and sits down again. Then she says something unexpected about England, something about being afraid of black men. He says it's daft to be afraid, and goes on to spend an unusually long time explaining how nobody is afraid of them. He calls them darkies. When he is finished she mentions something else she is afraid of in England, only this time she is making it up. By doing this several times she gets him to say lots of things about England, things I didn't think about before like going to school by bus or on the underground train. For a minute I want to go there straight away, just to see if everything is as I picture it now. When she can't get him to go on talking any longer, she pieces together the whole plan and lists all the things that have to be done before we leave. My father stands in the middle of the kitchen unsure what to do. Bríd says that it will all turn out for the best in the end. But the plan just stands there, separate from everything that has ever happened.

Soon we are all busy getting ready to go see him off. On the way to the station he sits in the front seat of the hackney car leaning forward with the knuckles of his left hand pressed white against the dashboard. He stares ahead to where the hedges loop over the road, all weighed down with brambles and softened with dandelion fluff and bits of hay combed from passing carts. Bríd tries to talk to him, reminding him that as soon as he gets the flat he will see us all again, for definite. Then she settles into a different position, waits for a few seconds and begins in a half-hearted way to say the same thing again. But her voice gets light, almost weightless and she stops. I do not want to be there listening to all this and remembering the other journeys to the station, with the same August hedges lurching in over the road and then the same platform, checking things, filling in, replacing, saying it all again – waiting.

I climb the steps of the footbridge, two at a time, glad to be away up there over the tracks watching out for the train. Bríd makes a big fuss about not letting my sisters follow me. I'm first to see the train and when I tell them, the talking starts again – all lively as if that's how it had been the whole time. As the noise of the train fills the station Bríd and my father raise their voices, smiling almost as if they are pleased with the way the clamour of the train overpowers them, making it impossible to say anything except 'careful, look after yourself, bye'. And Bríd says a last goodbye in a low voice, below the noise level of the train engine, wrapping it all up, just in time, a few weeks, for definite. At most a month or so.

On the way home she is half smiling and at the same time sort of crying in a way that most people wouldn't notice. She asks the hackney man to stop in the town for choc-ices for us.

3

On the following Monday we go back to school. Bríd writes a note to my teacher, Mrs Clyne, saying that I will not be getting the new school books because 'the family is going to England'. Hegarty comes with me as far as the school gate but instead of going in he goes over to the farmers' cars parked at the far side of the road. There are three of them there waiting to hire lads from the school to pull beet for the day. Babs pretends not to know that whenever the farmers are there Hegarty misses school. But I'm certain she asks him for the money when he gets back in and always gives him a note for the teacher next day saying he was sick.

As soon as school is over I go with the others to the hurling field. The trainer Tom Behan is already there, walking up and down the side line, talking to Fonsie Dineen who is part of everything that goes on in the town. Tom Behan shouts instructions across at us, still talking to Dineen and hiking his trousers up without taking his hands out of his pockets.

At the end of the practice Tom Behan calls me over. On the way I try and keep a face that shows I have no idea that he wants me to be captain. His lower lip is drawn over the upper one and when he speaks his mouth opens like a cage hatch, letting out words that have got jerky, like animals in captivity.

'Not much point, is there?'

'Not much point in you coming here any more.'

'Not much point, well from what I hear anyway. Is there? From what I hear you're off to England.'

I wait, without saying a word, still thinking he is going to ask me to be the captain. Then I feel my whole face burning and hear myself asking him if I should come to the next practice match.

'When are you off?'

'The end of the month, probably.'

'You can do what you like so, do whatever you like.'

The future cuts through the moment like a blade. Tom Behan walks away, leaving Fonsie Dineen there staring at me. He smiles, but the crimson blotches on his face which have nearly all joined together make his smile frightening. As I turn to walk towards the gate he asks me if I want a lift home.

'I'm going right to your very door.'

He has a big blue Ford Consul and as we drive through the town everyone salutes or nods. Fonsie Dineen is an auctioneer and has a dance band as well. They have played on nearly every stage in Ireland, but hardly ever play now because two years ago the accordionist died of a stroke. It was at a wedding in Kilkenny and afterwards everybody said he wasn't able for the rock 'n' roll and that Fonsie Dineen should have known that.

'So you're off to England? A great place. You'll have everything you want there. All free, schools, hospitals, houses, all there for the taking.'

He looks over at me and then quickly looks back at the road ahead. I know he wants me to say something but I don't know what it is I'm supposed to say.

'Any harm in asking you what is going to happen to the house when you leave?'

I don't answer straight away because I'm trying to imagine other people living in it. He asks the question again, but in a different way. Friendlier. This time I say I don't know.

He pushes himself back against the seat until his arms are in a straight line from his shoulders to the steering wheel. Then he looks at me sort of sideways. He thinks that I don't notice what he is doing because when I look over at him he smirks like someone who has been caught doing something sneaky. Suddenly he starts speaking in a loud voice.

'Times are good, bedad times are good. Off to England? Times are good. When I was your age I was working fourteen hours a day, starting at six in the morning, lighting fires. Five fires in the winter, that's how many I had to have lit by half-seven in the morning, and enough fuel beside each one to last until they all went to bed.'

I push my fingers into the creases in the shiny red vinyl seat and scrape up crumbs and dust with my nails. Each time he pauses I hope that he has stopped talking, but he goes on telling me how terrible it was when he was young. He curves his hands around the steering wheel letting them fall gradually until they reach the lowest point and then steering the car with his thumbs, tells me I'm lucky. With that he gives an Oh-Boy headshake and starts off again.

'Five fires in all.'

He smirks.

'Well here we are at your very door.'

I grow suddenly weary, overpowered by the thought of leaving.

The old men on Moratorium Row take stock of us in a

slow, drawn out way, so slow and drawn out that their gaze is almost hypnotic. Dineen walks over to talk to them and I stand there thinking about the question Dineen asked me about our house. In the corner of my eye I glimpse Hegarty. Somehow I had not seen him when we drove up a minute before. He walks up to me and without saying anything pushes his hand towards my face, opening it to reveal three coins. He quickly closes it and runs away. All at once the thoughts from which I'm racing catch up with me and I'm forced to think about the way the day at the castle ended with the sound of swarming crows drowning out a voice saying I do not want to go.

I leave my bag in the hallway and go back out.

As Dineen approaches Moratorium Row two of the old men take their caps off. Another one, John Joe Mackey, goes to stand up but Dineen, with his hand outstretched, rushes over, saving him from easing himself off the wall.

'Anything strange?'

They look about a bit and then look at each other. The oldest of them, Fran Dooley, makes a few shocking predictions about the weather and for a while it seems like they are all going to start talking. But they don't have anything much to say to each other so they just take turns to say 'aye' every so often. When his turn comes, Dineen says 'aye' too, but then he asks them if they remember the night, the famous night, during the fight for independence when he was a houseboy in the Forestocks and set Mrs Forestock on fire. The old men let on that they have to be reminded of what happened so Dineen imitates Mrs Forestock running around the room in flames, grabbing all the photographs of her husband and her son.

For that moment they are men of purpose again, remembering a time when all the talk was about freedom with everyone going about telling each other how great things were going to be. There is a low rumble of pleasure on Moratorium

Row. But as it gives way to the usual peering and waiting, Dineen skelps away like a spider and before the old men realize he has left he is knocking on our door.

Bríd answers the door almost immediately and I know by the way she smiles with her lips drawn closely together that she is pleased to see him, maybe even proud. Dineen stands to the side of the doorway and starts telling her about how good I am at hurling. Everything he says sort of explodes in front of him, then just dangles in mid air. The odd word travels as far as the old men and as it reaches them they lift their heads like tortoises.

'Off to England – I hear.'

Bríd moves her fingers through her hair, bulking it to the side as she prepares to answer him. But before she says anything he starts telling her the same things about England as he told me.

'Free schools, hospitals, houses, all there for the taking, truly a land of opportunity. When are you off?'

'The end of the month.'

Dineen puts on a very serious face, scrunching up his fore-head, his eyes and his nose, drawing them all down together.

'It would be in your best interest, and I'm not just saying this, to put the house here on the books in the office.' He points over in the general direction of the town as if we don't know where his office is.

Even though Bríd agrees immediately he still goes on to tell her all about the people who have gone to England and put their houses on his books and how there will always be people looking for houses. She thanks him for coming all the way out and then tells him that she had intended asking his advice about the house anyway. With one hand waving well above his head he walks to the gate, where with a quick head flick he turns back.

'I'll have the place let or sold for you before you know it. As Kingo Bingo says, if you don't bet you sure won't get.'

As he gets into his car he shouts 'All the best' at the old men, revs the engine impatiently and swings out onto the low road to the town.

*

At the beginning of the following week a letter comes from my father saying that he has found a flat that will do for the time being. There and then Bríd decides to leave on Saturday week and there and then I think to myself that Friday week will be my last day at school. I keep thinking of how it will be a completely different sort of day. But it turns out to be the same as every other except for the prayer Mrs Clyne makes everyone say for me and my family. I'm not sure if it is right to be praying for myself so I just say bits of the prayer and then say the Amen part in a very definite way. After that Mrs Clyne, looking directly at me, starts singing 'Hail Queen of Heaven the Ocean Star'. Slowly we all join in.

When I get home from school my sisters are counting rows of acorns on the front doorstep. They are all dressed up. For a minute I think the plans have been changed and we are going today instead of tomorrow. When they see me they jump up and start telling me I have to change into the new clothes I got for going to England because Queenie, and here they both draw their breath together, because Queenie has told Bríd to bring us to her house to say goodbye and have our tea. On the way into the kitchen I get ready to tell Bríd I'm not wearing my new shiny trousers. But when I walk in she just stays staring out the window and in a very quiet voice asks me about school and about what Mrs Clyne said. Then in an even quieter voice she tells me to change into my new clothes. I want to say no but her voice withers to a whisper as though everything has already been decided.

The table in Queenie's is all set out. In the middle there is a plate of buns, each one in its own paper holder, covered with pink icing. On top of the icing there are speckled grains of coloured crumbs and in the centre, a silver ball set in a twist of dark pink icing. Beside this plate of buns is a bowl of green jelly with bits of orange set into it like goldfish frozen in a pond.

Bríd smiles but stops suddenly. She tells Queenie that there is still a lot to be done before we go. Queenie says nothing so Bríd smiles again. We stand at the door, staring at the table. Queenie looks at us and shaking her head slowly tells us that nothing on the table can be touched before four o'clock. Then, pointing her finger over at the low round clock on the mantelpiece, she says four o'clock again and adds 'not a minute before'. After that she just stands there looking at us for a long time. Her eyes are open as far as they can go and her mouth is closed so firmly that her lips have almost disappeared. Bríd starts talking about Babs and the round-about way she was asking for the things we are not bringing to England with us. Queenie is nodding her head and cutting in every few seconds to say, 'what can you expect anyway'. Suddenly there is a crash and before anyone can think anything about it, we are all standing around the broken figure of the Child of Prague statue, the largest part of which is still shaking. Very quickly Queenie walks over to the table, her eyelids drawn almost fully over her eyes. She picks up one setting – a spoon, a bowl and a plate – and carries them carefully over to the sideboard.

'Time for your tea now.'

It's not nearly four, but I don't say anything because I know that there is something fishy going on. We walk over to the table while Bríd picks up all the big bits of the Child of Prague.

'Not you,' Queenie hisses at Gretta as she grabs her by the shoulder.

Bríd beckons me to sit down as Queenie guides Gretta over to the corner taking a chair over with her. And there, sitting facing Gretta, she starts describing how much Agnes and I are enjoying everything.

'I didn't do it, it wasn't me,' Gretta starts to cry.

'I'll teach you not to tell lies to me, you brazen little bitch.'

Without any warning Agnes jumps up from the table and runs over to Bríd, leaving me there, slowly breaking the pink icing away from the edge of a bun. Before I think about what I'm doing I turn and tell Queenie that Gretta didn't do it.

Queenie's face uncrumples and for a second or two I think that she believes me. But just as I start to say that the statue fell by itself her face sharpens, shooting out full of points and edges.

'You are a liar too. Now, get out. Go. All of you, this minute, I never want to see any of you. Ever again.'

With that she jumps up, pushes Gretta back into the corner and rushes out of the room. Bríd lifts Agnes up into her arms because she has started to scream. Gretta is afraid to move from the corner. Bríd has to tell her not to be upset lots of times and then we leave. I'm glad we're going to England tomorrow.

In the morning I lie in bed listening to Bríd moving about downstairs. Some of the sounds are unfamiliar. Out there, waiting to be touched is the thought that today we are going to England. I remember again in snatches, Hegarty falling from the ledge in the castle and the way I tumbled back in search of a moment when it was not happening. I think of what he said afterwards, about me not living around here any longer, and then the sound of crows and my father telling me about the swimming pools in England. Days, all leading to today, making this part of a memory before it ever begins. I'm afraid and still if I was to find out that we were no longer going, I know that it would be a big let-down.

On the way downstairs I see that the kitchen table has been moved into the hall and a whole pile of blankets and clothes have been piled up on top of it. Underneath is a box with all the Christmas decorations in it. I ask Bríd if we are going to bring it with us. She stops to think for a second.

'No, for all you know we might end up coming home for Christmas.'

I cannot think of any family that has gone to England and come home for Christmas. All the same, I begin to imagine us arriving home on Christmas Eve with presents for all the people we know.

'But once you get used to things over there you won't want to come home.'

I nod and with less certainty she says, 'anyway there won't be all that much to come home to'. In that moment all my thoughts about England surface, forming – one beside the next – like one of those postcards showing a whole lot of different views of a place, the underground trains, Queen Elizabeth, motorways, swimming pools. Then Bríd, with her voice full of certainty again, says she is sure everything will turn out for the best in the end.

4

All morning there are people calling in. Babs stands at the stove making tea for them and when they are going Bríd tells them that we will be coming home in a few months for Christmas – probably. She says that we are just going to see what it's like over there, if it is all that it is cracked up to be.

Babs leaves when we have finished our dinner and from then on nobody comes into the house, but they stay outside waiting to wish us well when we are leaving. The old men begin to move from Moratorium Row, slowly making their way over to the embankment opposite our house. When they have settled there the wellwishers drift across the road and gather around them. I watch from my bedroom window. I know them all but there is something unfamiliar about the way they just look at our house, saying almost nothing to each other. When Bríd walks out to the gate with a belted suitcase they stop talking all together. She leaves the suitcase beside two boxes which are wrapped in brown paper and very tightly tied with fawn twine. Some people arrive on bicycles and leave them down at Babs' house. I watch them walking up, not realizing until they sit down on the embankment with the others, that they have come to see us off.

Bríd hangs a string bag full of shoes on the gate. My hurley is pushed into the middle of it. She nods when one of the old men, his face veined and lumpy like a cabbage, says something to her.

A thinnish black and white dog comes trotting down the path. When it stops at the gate I notice it has a plum-like lump sticking out from its ribs. One of the wellwishers shouts at it but it pretends not to notice. Then one of them, whose own sheepdog is running up and down at the far side of the green, whistles. The sheepdog comes immediately and is pointed at the mongrel which, in spite of all the shouting, goes on sniffing the parcels. But as the dark bony sheepdog approaches with its head low, the black and white dog skulks away, full of shame and slyness. Suddenly, bristling about the neck and above the ears, it stops. They are both staring sideways at each other, neither moving an inch. Then with one great leap the sheepdog fixes its teeth into the other dog's neck. Some of the wellwishers run to separate them. The sheepdog releases its grip, only to start a new attack and regrip the other dog by the upper jaw and the eye socket. I clench my fist and draw breath through my teeth, feeling the mince of crackling knuckle. The sheepdog lets go and stiffens to its full size, like a statue celebrating its own victory.

The wellwishers examine the injured dog which is pushing its snout into the wall and moving backwards with pain, edging towards the suitcase and the parcels.

'Take her out of her misery.'

Lots of people agree, all at once, 'yeah, take her out of her misery'.

Without looking at the others, one of the men raises his foot. My foot moves back too. I try to keep it back but I am unable to hold out against the force with which the man drives his foot into the dog's stomach. Behind him one of the other wellwishers comes running with a large rock and, lifting it high above his head, aims it at the dog's skull.

The hackney car arrives and Bríd walks out carrying a Travelight bag. She says something to the driver and then rushes back inside to get the rest of the luggage. Standing at the bottom of the stairs she calls me. I wait before telling her that I'm coming. The room is empty and feels as though it has just filled with cold air. My voice echoes thinly around and around and I say I'm coming again, just to hear my voice echo again. I take all the bits and scraps of things, useless things, from the window ledge and stuff them into my pocket, overpowered for a moment by a wish to take everything I can see.

'Coming, I'm coming.'

My sisters are running in and out of the kitchen, spitting lemonade at each other. As Bríd walks out the door she turns and with a gleaming smile asks us if we have left anything behind. And that moment breaks out of the time rut to become the memory around which all other memories of going to England cluster.

Everything Bríd says to me in the hackney car is followed by 'please', all tight and clipped. The hackney man says that it is not a bad day and she takes so long to answer him that he looks in the mirror to see if there is something wrong. Nobody speaks again until we turn the corner at the top of Main Street. The hackney man looks at us in the mirror before he speaks.

'There's holy murder going on here today.'

Bríd says 'oh', coughs a little and says 'oh' again, this time louder and much clearer.

'Yep. Holy murder. On account of the Laughlins getting the television into the bar.' Before he continues he turns round and looks at us.

'Yep. The committee hired two buses to go to the match tomorrow. Laughlin didn't say anything to anyone about getting the television in until yesterday and when people heard, some of them said they wouldn't be going to the match at all, that instead they would watch it in Laughlins' on the television. Well, you don't have to ask what happened.'

He waits for Bríd to reply but she says nothing.

'Yep. Dineen and Behan and two others on the committee walked into Laughlins' yesterday and told Laughlin that if the crowd who were supposed to be coming from Portlaoise to put up the aerial came, they would, well Dineen at any rate, would pull it down with his own hands.'

He pauses but is no longer expecting us to join in.

'And what's more he would, a right boyo when he's crossed, the same Dineen.'

Our train will pass the whole way back alongside the road we have just travelled, skirting the edge of the moor before it slowly curves out into the open country.

'You mightn't agree with me but the television is here to stay and every pub in the town will have one before Christmas as well as all the houses. And the Hogan Stand will be empty next year. Mark my words. Last January, just after Christmas, they showed the final from the year before, the '62 match, bits of it anyway. I drove a crowd from the town here to see it in Roscrea. All the goals were in slow motion.'

The hackney man pulls up outside Laughlins' pub where small groups of people have gathered. With the engine running he rolls down the window and asks if there have been any new moves. They all point to the roof where Laughlin and his brothers are guarding the new aerial, holding on to the chimney stack. We look up and for a minute I forget why we're sitting in the car, only to begin the journey again, falling back as the hackney car swerves out and away down Main Street to the station.

If it was winter or early spring with the hedges all thinned out and spindly we would probably be able to see the tops of the houses on our side of the green from the train. I saw them last year when I went on the school tour to Dublin.

The last time I was over near the railway line was a week or so before school re-opened. As we drive up beside the station I think about the plan we had to storm the green that morning and free everyone.

Bríd has the money to pay the hackney man all ready. He examines the coins and picks out an English two shilling piece which he folds into my hand.

'For luck,' he says smiling.

On the train Bríd asks me questions to which she definitely knows the answers. I do not feel like answering. It reminds me of the way she sometimes talks to me when my father is home, asking me questions just for the sake of it. Several times she asks me who has the tickets, her or me. Each time I search my pockets even though I know that she has them. By the time I'm finished searching for them and about to tell her she has them she is busy doing something else, tightening the bow from which Agnes's ringlets curl, brushing the collar of her coat, even asking new questions. Far away, I see the wall flicker through the gaps in the hedge.

The train stops at every station. All the buildings are alike, grey with high, pointed roofs. Most of the people who get on the train have tan cardboard suitcases. Some of them have parcels too, just like us. At one station there are hundreds of people. The man across the way from us tells the woman beside him that all these people were brought by another train and left there waiting for the boat train. She says it's a disgrace that they have to wait like that.

There is a man making his way through the crowd to the train, swaying from side to side. As he moves forward people step out of his way. Bríd tells us not to stare at him because he is drunk. The woman across from us says it's a disgrace again.

The train goes right out to the edge of the sea where there are two huge ships waiting. They are so huge that I cannot imagine them moving. I turn to ask Bríd which one we will be going on. She says she is not sure.

We have so much luggage that we have to make the journey from the train to the boat in two stages. About half way between the two Bríd puts down the boxes and tells me to mind them while she goes back with Gretta and Agnes to collect the cases. The moving crowd divides as it approaches, all except for the drunk man who stops, winks at me and then falls back a bit. Afraid that he is going to say something to me, I turn around and watch as the empty space between the hordes of people and the boat gets smaller and smaller and then disappears like an island swallowed up by a big rolling wave.

Bríd leads the way up the ramp lifting the case and two boxes. I have another box, the Travelight and the string bag with the shoes and the hurley. Agnes and Gretta are holding hands and Bríd keeps on putting the case down and pulling them towards her. She says 'excuse me' lots of times to the man in the blue and white uniform who helps her over the final hump saying 'this way to the passenger lounge, madame'. Once we get seats Agnes starts crying but Bríd pays no attention to her. She is listening to the people around and I know by the way her forehead and eyes are moving that she is frightened of something. There are lots of people shouting to one another up and down the crowded passageway. The ones at our end are trying to tell the ones at the entrance that they have seats kept for them. They all have English accents. Without warning, Bríd stands up and bending over towards me whispers that she thinks we are in the first class lounge. Her hands are shaking. She looks around for signs but there are none except a big long list of what to do in an emergency. Still looking she grabs our luggage and starts to cut back through the crowd which is beginning to untangle. One of the buttons on her new turquoise coat snaps off as Gretta and Agnes are pushed backwards. Gretta asks her why we are leaving. Bríd looks at me and at first I think that she is blaming me for what happened, but it slowly begins to dawn on me that she wants me to decide what to do next. She wants me to be in charge. For the first time I feel part of something fragile, ashamed of all the times that day I tried to pretend I was on my own.

We find a seat outside on deck. It is dark. I want to say that we were not in the first class seats but instead I say that we should ask someone where the other seats are. Bríd takes over and we soon find ourselves back in the lounge we had left a few minutes before. The unfamiliar person who had begun to take shape in my mind disappears when I look at Bríd, sitting there clutching her handbag and smiling directly at me for the first time that day.

My sisters' faces flush with the heat and before long they are asleep. Bríd opens the top button of their coats. As she is doing this she turns towards me and says she hopes Queenie will sweep the hall floor and that she and Michael will take away the table and the other things soon.

Long before the boat arrives in Holyhead people begin to take their luggage out of the passenger lounge. Bríd fastens the buttons on my sisters' coats. They wake but do not move until Bríd reminds them that we are going to England. When nothing happens they fall asleep again. The next time they wake the noise of the boat engine has softened to a hum which fades altogether as the boat cranks and sways towards the pier. We gather under a sign which Gretta spells out bit by bit. Disembarkation. I am delighted to be arriving in England.

Word goes around that we are all at the wrong place. Someone says that it is not a door at all. Some people start to drift off but suddenly a big part of the ship seems to fall away and everyone spills out. We just move with the crowd, this time bringing all our luggage in one go, the belted suitcases, the boxes and the string bag of shoes with my hurley in the middle.

England. Bríd smiles. People hush each other so as to hear the voice on the loud speaker. All the trains are ready and waiting. I lead the way to our train, the express for London. Inside it is warm and steamy. There are cream covers on the bulging headrests. I sink into a soft navy seat and straight away think of Dineen's car.

After sitting there for a long time the train shunts out of the station. The windows reflect the windows on the opposite side, distorting the image of the passengers in the seats across the aisle from us. For a second I think I see Hegarty running alongside the train. Unwilling to let go of the thought, I imagine him tapping the window of the train shouting 'the best of luck'. His steps stretch to cover large sections of the platform as he strides forward from a past a lot less recent than yesterday afternoon. I try to remember if he came out to say goodbye and if he was there running beside the hackney car or the train shouting 'best of luck'. But I can barely remember what he looks like and the harder I try the further he backs into the past. I turn to ask Bríd if she saw Hegarty but the question disappears with the memory and is instantly replaced with another question.

'Where will they bury the dog?' I wait for her to answer but then see that she is not even thinking about the question.

'Will they bury it in our garden?' She says no. 'On the green?' She says no again. I lose interest but in between waves of tiredness I keep on saying new places and Bríd keeps on saying no.

5

When I wake the train is gliding gently. Some people have taken their luggage off the overhead racks and placed it on the tables. Slowly I realize we are about to arrive in Euston Station. Bríd is craning her neck towards the window, concentrating on her reflection as she draws a thin line of scarlet lipstick from one side of her upper lip to the other. She then rolls both her lips together and with a sudden backward jerk of her head examines herself, squinching her lips up into a tight bow. Through her reflection I see my father standing on the platform flanked by two people who look English. They wave as the train squeaks to a halt, shrieks and throws us back down onto our seats. My father keeps pointing at us but I'm not sure if they know who they are waving at. The woman has a fixed smile and a beehive hair-do which gives her a *Woman's Own* face. I climb from the train with Bríd telling us what to do and saying 'pleased to meet you' in a variety of tones.

The two people with my father walk towards us, their hands stretched out to help with the luggage. He lags behind a bit and seeing him there I am struck by how old he looks compared to the people he is with.

When Bríd says everything there is to say about the journey, they start telling us about the worst journey they have ever had on the boat, last year when they brought their caravan to Ireland. While the man sways from side to side to show us how rough the sea was, the woman turns, looks at Agnes and Gretta and says 'aren't you going to give Dad a big birdie?'

We all look at each other not sure what to do because nobody in our family ever says things like that.

Gretta and Agnes hide behind Bríd and my father picks up the luggage without speaking. I watch him walking away, unsettled by the thought that he is somehow not at the centre of things.

Lil and Gus Finnegan came to England the summer the war ended. When they speak they sound as if they are imitating each other. Anybody would think they were English with their manners and their full command of the railway station. Gus is wearing a blue anorak and a white polo neck jumper. Last summer he bought a house with thirty years left to run on the lease. Lil says it will see them through to the grave. Then she laughs. The house is divided into three flats with what he calls a sitting tenant in the top one. They live in the middle flat with Seamus and Noreen, their two children, who, Lil says, are well on their way. My father is renting the downstairs flat. They tell us he was the first to reply to their ad on the Club notice board. Behind us, Lil says she is sure we will like the flat. Bríd, smiling and nodding her head, says of course we will.

My father hands me the string bag. It's awkward to carry, the shoes bulge out to one side and the hurley keeps on toppling out. He says something about hurling but I let on not to hear. Lil leads the way, her high heels clacking and making a scraping noise every so often as she changes her pace with a little skip. She is wearing brown slacks and a type of jacket coat that I have never seen before. She knows all about England and everything we have to do to make a go of things. She turns around to speak but before she says whatever it was she was going to say she admires Bríd's coat. Bríd says that she bought it in Singleton's in the town and then begins to explain how the button came off. Lil stares at the coat for a moment before she starts telling us more things about England.

'Schools, mainly Protestant, have to be careful. Their names are down,' and pointing at my father she says, 'Gave them to me last week.'

My father nods and when he sees us all looking at him he nods again.

'It wasn't any bother. Shame and Noe go there. What am I talking about?' She raises her eyes. 'Noe goes there. Shame finished in July. He's an apprentice with an electrician now, a friend of Gus's. And their dates of birth, one Dan wasn't sure of, have to check it. The Social Services, not as good as they are made out to be. Look at this.'

She opens her mouth very wide and pulls down one side of her lip showing us a black and silver filling which she says bled for three years. Then she tells us about the Christmas raffle at the Club and the Christmas club at the Co-op.

'All your Christmas shopping paid for in advance, can you imagine?'

Even though Bríd is tired she still puts on a face that makes it look as if she can hardly imagine all the things she is hearing. But she is not able to stay looking like that because Lil goes on speaking in a way that makes it seem as if she is always just about to get to the most important part of what she is talking about.

'Nobody makes the pud in England. What is the point, for God's sake, in slaving like that with all the suet and everything when you can buy it made up and three-quarters cooked.'

She looks at my father expecting him to tell Bríd that all the things she is saying about the Christmas pud are right, but he says nothing, so she turns to Gus.

'You much prefer the Co-op pud, don't you?'

Gus puts on a very serious voice.

'Honestly, Dan, you won't spot the difference. The first time Lil got the Co-op pud she said nothing about it until after I'd finished my third helping. When I heard where it had come from I was taken by surprise. It came from the Co-op and straight away I said that we'd have the same one the following Christmas. And we have been having them ever since. That's at least ten years now. About ten years isn't it Lil, since the first time we had the Co-op pud?'

'You must be joking, it's more than ten, much more, the children were small, I remember they were small.'

I feel the skin on my knuckles stretch as I tighten my grip on the handle of the bag I am carrying, wishing with all my will that Bríd would just agree to get the pud when Christmas comes. But she just keeps on a face that shows how thankful she is for what they are doing for us. Then as if by a miracle, Lil turns to me and tells me that Shame and Noe wouldn't have any other kind of Christmas pud. Straight away I say that it sounds as though we'll be having it too – when Christmas comes. I think it will all end at that, but it doesn't.

'That's one of the worst things about Ireland. You can get nothing made up like that. You have to do everything yourself and sometimes the shops don't even have what you want. Last summer we stopped in one place where they hadn't even heard of some of the things we were asking for, ordinary things, can't think of what they were now, but ordinary everyday things. Looked at us as if we were fools.'

We all squeeze into their Ford Anglia. Lil sits in the front with Gus and, full of certainty, starts telling us about herself. When she looks around and sees how carefully we are listening she starts using a different voice, quieter, less sure.

She tells us that she remembers exactly what it was like when she and Gus arrived in England, listing all the reasons it turned out to be such a good move. She says she cannot understand how anyone would want to live in Ireland.

'I'd sooner live in Russia with the Communists and the cold. I'll never forget how cold it was, outside at the back of the dance hall in Cashel. It's colder over there, colder than here I mean, not Russia. Himself here wasn't thinking of the cold and I hardly knew what was going on. Well one thing led to another, if you know what I mean. He calls it the flight into Egypt. The flight into Egypt is right. Can we drive down to show them what we had to live in when we came over first, temporary accommodation is what the Council called it. A dump is what I call it, though to be honest with you I was glad of it at the time. You should see our Shamie now, big as a house.'

Lil looks over at Gus who smiles and says 'that's right'. His sleek hair is combed into a mane, curling a little over his white polo neck. The Brylcreem and petrol fumes mix. Agnes and Gretta whisper to Bríd that they feel sick but I sit forward, listening. Bríd and my father sit upright and say nothing.

Gus keeps on saying how unusual it is to drive through London at fifty miles an hour and tells us we should see the streets on weekdays. Every time we stop at a traffic light he pretends to be thrown forward a bit and then turns around and smiles with half his face. He keeps pointing things out. Landmarks. Driving slowly down one street he points up towards the tall white houses and tells us that that's where the Permissive Society lives. We all tilt our heads but we can see nobody because the curtains are drawn in most of the houses.

We stop outside a church and I have to remind myself again that it is Sunday. The Mass going on inside is nearly over so we stay for the first half of the one that follows. On the way out Lil tells Bríd that there is a lot less fuss about Mass in England. And pointing down at her legs asks Bríd if she could imagine wearing slacks to Mass in Ireland.

The way she keeps using the word Ireland makes me feel like a cheat.

Just as Gus is about to start up the engine again he looks at his watch and tells Lil that as soon as the Mass we have left is over the Club will be opening. Without thinking for a second Lil says we will wait. Then they spend the next twenty minutes telling us about the Club and the people we will be meeting. Gretta and Agnes fall asleep. Bríd and my father stare at the people passing by. They are holding onto the jolt straps even though we are not moving.

The Club is directly opposite the church but the entrance to it is down a long narrow lane by the side. Sons of Érin is written overhead and surrounded by a whole series of entwined lines which end in snakes' heads. The É of Érin is almost lost in a blaze of colour. Inside there are tall windows with wide sills packed tight with hundreds of souvenir dolls and leprechauns. Lil explains that it is a tradition, when people go home on holiday they bring back a memento for the Club as well as sending a postcard. She points to the other side of the room where a thin red-faced man is polishing glasses. Behind him there are more postcards than I have ever seen. Millions. He waves at us and Lil leads us all over and tells him we are just off the boat.

'God, I didn't even know Dan had a family, not to mention the fact that he was bringing them over.'

We look at each other and Bríd starts blushing, but before anyone else sees this she bends down to unfasten the top button of Agnes's coat.

'Well Dan, aren't you the glick one, what'll it be? The usual?'

My father nods and asks for lemonade for us. Then he asks Gus and Lil what they would like to drink. Gus draws his lips

46

together into a straight line and curves his eyebrows up as if he finds it difficult to decide what to drink. My father doesn't ask Bríd what she would like but when Lil asks for a Baby-cham, Bríd says she'll have one too. Gretta and Agnes fall asleep on the same chair and Bríd has to wake them up when the lemonade comes.

After Mass, lots of people arrive. They are all talking very fast and the men are clasping their hands and rubbing them together. Lil calls several of them over and pointing at us tells them who we are. When her Babycham arrives she clinks glasses with Bríd and then, holding her glass high in the air, wishes us the best of luck.

More and more drinks arrive and by the middle of the afternoon the table in front of us is so full of glasses and bottles that another table has to be moved across to take the overflow.

'Turn on the television for them.'

I look around to see where the voice came from but there are at least six people looking at me, smiling, all waiting for the television to be turned on. When it is they go on looking at us.

'Well? Is it what you thought it would be like?'

I think the man is talking to me but I'm not sure because he has a squint. He says 'well' again and so I answer.

'There are televisions at home and in Dublin there are lots of them.'

He fixes my father with one of his eyes, the bulging one, and me with the other which is tight and watery.

'You might have a bit of a smart-alec on your hands there Dan.'

Only when Lil speaks do I begin to see that I have said something wrong.

'They've had televisions at home for over a year now, it's easy known that you haven't been back in a while.'

The man looks at Lil with his big eye and at Bríd with his

47

small one. Both begin to speak to him together, Lil giving way first.

'... and then the nuns in the town hired one for the week the Kennedys came. They put it up on the altar stand between the two blackboards and everyone was asked in to see it.'

I cut in and tell him that we all clapped at the end when it was turned off.

I want to stop talking but somehow I am unable, sort of afraid of what is going to happen when I stop. So I just go on telling him and the others who are listening about the television in the convent and the clapping when Mr Dunne turned it off and how Mr Dunne cleaned the yard in the convent and sometimes did other jobs too. Lil interrupts to tell everyone how much she hates nuns and I jump at the chance to stop talking.

I think there is some sort of news programme on television but it is hard to make out because the barman is standing in front of it, blocking most of it out. He speaks without turning around.

'It is usually Laurel and Hardy or something like that at this time on a Sunday.'

Each time he turns the knob the picture breaks up. Sometimes it is all grains and lines and sometimes it is just a white fuzz. Then he turns another knob and a clear picture wobbles onto the screen. I know it's about Berlin because the voice says Checkpoint Charlie. There are rows and rows of people. Nearly all of them have children holding onto them and they look at us as if we shouldn't be looking at them.

Gus smacks his lips before he sips his stout and while he is drinking he looks about the room and then at the television.

'Isn't it awful in Berlin? Lucky we stayed neutral during the war.'

Everyone agrees and then out of the blue Bríd says a number, following quickly with a series of other numbers. Lil starts telling us about the pools but Bríd is not listening, she is saying the numbers in a singsong voice, insisting that they were the numbers on the inside page of my grandmother's ration book. Lil leans across and some of her Babycham spills across the table. She says 'Jesus' in a loud voice and people look over at her first and then at us. Bríd says the numbers again, this time slowly as if she was trying to remember them. Before anyone has time to say anything about what's going on, she is crying, and I don't want to watch. Neither does my father. Lil stands up and tells Bríd that she will bring her over to the toilets. Several people are staring but all Bríd does is say the numbers again and again. On the way Lil points to the notice board and to the advertisement for the flat we are going to live in. It's hanging to one side and I think that Lil is going to straighten it but she pulls it off.

'Can't have people thinking it's still to let.'

Gretta and Agnes run up to Bríd, but instead of going over to the toilets they all walk out the main door together.

The man with the bulging eye looks at the door and at my father.

'You might have trouble on your hands there Dan. She might be as well off at home. That's what I think anyway, and it's why I have me own there.'

My father says nothing. But Gus, putting his empty glass down, says Ireland is all right for a holiday but that nobody can make a living there and it is run by priests.

We spend the rest of the afternoon driving around London, looking at the places that Gus and Lil once lived in. And although Gus says that there is no point in going to see the very first place they stayed in, a hostel, because it's now demolished, we eventually end up going to look at the new houses built on the site. Lil tells us that it was infested with rats and very unsuitable for a young couple expecting a baby. Another place they lived in had been so badly damaged in the blitz that only the basement, which they got for nothing, was considered in any way safe.

49

Bríd says she is sorry we are putting them to so much trouble. They both answer together and say 'not at all' and go on to say that they often spend Sundays looking at all the places they once lived in and that it's nice to have someone to show it all to once in a while.

At about half past five we pull up outside a house with a caravan parked in the front garden.

'Bet you're wondering how it got there? See,' Gus says, stretching his arms out in an effort to show that the garden gate is no wider than the front door.

We all stand looking at the problem and after a very long time Gus, moving his arms about like a magician, explains. He speaks with such certainty that his mouth clamps between each word.

'Simple. Hacksaw. Cut. The railings – simple?'

The words follow us into the house.

We look at everything and Bríd, with a voice I do not recognize, keeps saying how nice it all is, while at the same time telling Agnes and Gretta to stop touching things.

The tin-opener is attached to the wall which Lil says is not that common in England and unheard of in Ireland.

When Lil finally leaves we look around and my father lights the gas and sets about making tea. There are two packets of pink wafer biscuits on the table. Bríd says she is sure it will all turn out for the best and he says yes. I can't imagine how the tight spaces between the things they say to each other could ever be calm and unguarded. But when she tastes the tea she says that she prefers it to Babycham any day and my father, taking a small bottle wrapped in a brown paper bag from his pocket, smiles and as he pours it into his tea, tells her what the man with the bulging eye said about her. Then they both laugh and while they are still laughing there is a knock at the door.

'I just thought you'd like these, I'll call back later to help you fill them in.'

Lil walks in and hands Bríd applications forms for Irish dancing classes.

There are two bedrooms in the flat and the bigger of them is partitioned by a large wardrobe. On one side of this wardrobe is my bed, which faces the window. My sisters sleep in a double bed on the other side. From my bed I can see straight into the caravan because the lounge window of the caravan is only inches away from the bedroom window.

I want to stay awake and think about it all, but I have come to the end. I'm tired beyond any tiredness I ever felt before. Still, I fight sleep. I want to hold on to the excitement I felt leaning into the front of the Finnegans' car, listening, mesmerized by the future they conjured up for us.

The only thing threatening that future was my father's reluctance to be drawn into the discussion. Nothing the Finnegans said made him sit up. At first, I was hardly aware of it because he was, as he nearly always was with us, silent. But as the day wore on I began to suspect that he was deliberately refusing everything the Finnegans were offering. I didn't understand why and I certainly didn't want them to think that I was doing the same thing. So I took every chance I got to dissociate myself from him. These chances did not come up very often because Lil and Gus had so much to say, we talked very little among ourselves. But my father did ask me a few questions. Each time I only barely answered him, hoping that the Finnegans would take note. I didn't care what he thought about the offhand way I spoke. I wanted to push him aside. I wanted him out of the way. But every now and then and in a distant sort of way, his silence became a warning, and while it did not stop me in my gallop forward it certainly slowed me down a bit.

part two

6

In the weeks and months that followed I came to understand
that if my father ever did look forward it was to a time when
we would all return home. Nothing else held any future for
him. We would not be going home, at least not there and
then, so he spent his time looking back, holding on tightly to
anything he could grasp from that world. Whenever he talked
he talked about home. If he entered a conversation on any
other topic he would visibly lose interest before it got under
way.

I could and sometimes did drift back there with him,
answering his questions, remembering details which he would
then slowly piece together like a jigsaw. The difficulty was
that while he and I spoke about the same people, he was
removed from them in a way that I wasn't. For him, all the
people we knew were set into an unchanging story. Every time
he spoke about them they did and said exactly the same thing.

I wasn't able to think about home in that way. I wasn't able to focus on any of the people there for more than an instant. Sometimes I couldn't even remember their faces. Still, in some secret way, I must have held onto them because often, when I was doing something completely different, they would loom up and startle me with some expression or movement, so vivid, that for a sliver of time I lost all sense of being away from them. If I tried to hold onto them they just distorted themselves, taking on the voice or maybe the face of someone else. And while I stared at what they had become they scampered away to wherever it was they stayed. They seemed to have wills all of their own.

The same happened with places, like the green. It was a place I knew in every possible way. Still, whenever I tried to think about it, several images crowded in at once and I could not hold onto any of them. It might appear as a great flooded plain or completely covered in snow. Or it could become a windswept wasteland with the big tree flung, leafless, on its side and the old men moving among its roots like Neanderthals among the bones of a great dinosaur. It could just as easily merge with the moor, float away or become one big island with thousands of tobacco-coloured irises all wide open in the festering afternoon heat. It could and did become anything and everything. The only thing it would not do was stay still. So, as often as not, in those first months in England, my answers to my father's cautious questions about home amounted to little more than yes or no. Sometimes he would go on half-questioning me and sometimes he would just nod and sit there in silence.

That silence, I thought, marked the end of whatever conversation was going on. But I soon became aware that, like the nods that always preceded them, my father's silences were by no means alike. His nods were the clues and it was from these that I learned to interpret the silences that followed. There were the straightforward nods, the yeses, recognizable because they were much faster than any of the others. Then there was the slow mysterious bow which seemed to close the gates on a world of wisdom and bring everything to an unexpected halt. That nod was often followed by a drawn out, barely audible, intake of breath. But the one which made me feel very uneasy, made me feel as though I was somehow letting him down, was the nod of exasperation. It always followed when I answered one of his questions about home by saying I did not know or wasn't sure, abandoning him to search on his own.

I cannot pinpoint the moment when I first sensed that there was disappointment in that nod. But I do remember being aware of it on those Saturday mornings during that first winter, when he would bring me across London to the Inter Club hurling matches. We made the journey in two stages, first a bus ride that took over an hour and then a shorter journey on the tube. It was mostly on those bus journeys from Streatham to South Kensington station, that I began to mould the world I had left into a shape I hoped would stop him drifting into defeated silence. I didn't set out in any definite way to do that, it just seemed the only way around the discomfort I felt when he kept trying to talk about home.

It always started out in the same way, with me looking out the bus window, and continuing to look out even after I heard that lone 'well' which marked the beginning of the trek back. He would follow through with a name; Babs, Dineen, anyone. I would resist by pretending that what he had said was just by the way. But he persisted until awkwardly and very self-consciously, I would add some detail or other, maybe about Dineen's car or the practice matches. Before long, the talk focused on the hurling or something like that, with my half-answers following his broken questions. It could hardly be called a conversation because it rarely moved at a conversational pace and after each phrase or sentence we returned to occupy the separate worlds we lived in, his fixed and all arranged to his own liking and mine, uncharted and constantly on the move.

I'm not sure why I resisted answering those meandering questions. I think it was to do with the feeling that something which I wanted to hold onto was being prised from me. I wanted to put my fingers in my ears as he seized my replies. I did not want to listen to him repeating those replies, no matter how short, drifting away with them and lingering on the words as though for that moment, a brilliant light had been thrown on something he had been unable to see clearly for a very long time. He would then weave whatever it was I had said into one of his own memories of home, quickening the pace at which he spoke, asking me to repeat some detail, changing things around, all the time trying to shore up a world that went on collapsing. Still, he must have imagined that he was bringing it all to life because his face lost that tightness which usually kept his eyes squinched up.

There were rewards for joining my father on those journeys, rewards I not only enjoyed but in time set out to win. I loved the pride with which he spoke about me in the after Mass chat in the Club. Surrounded by men with whom my father felt wholly at home, I became the person I had wanted to be, the captain of the under-fourteens, the greatest loss to the county that the trainer could remember. 'A fact which,' my father pointed out one Sunday morning, 'would be obvious to anyone who knew that he had been asked to play for the under-sixteens the previous summer.' Then full of indignation, so as to disguise the baldness of his claim, he added, 'And him only thirteen at the time.' Before he finished telling them this he was looking at me, pleading with me to become part of the conspiracy. I wanted to, but despite myself I turned away from him, unnerved not so much by the lie, but by the wild-faced way he said the word 'thirteen'. I was afraid of what I saw in him but at the same time, I was drawn towards him, unused to thinking of him as someone on my side.

I held onto moments like that because I was at the centre of them and because I knew that as those Sunday afternoons moved towards evening he would grow silent and his silence would seep into everything that went on in the flat, slowly bringing things to a standstill. By night time I would begin to wonder if I had imagined his pride and admiration earlier that day.

Even though I stopped going to the Inter Club hurling matches with him and avoided talking about home, I sensed that during that first year a lot of what I knew and felt about the world I had left had become part of my father's story. But I saw no danger in that. I thought that my own story was there waiting to be told – in my own words – if I wanted to tell it. It did not occur to me for a moment that every time I followed my father back there, however reluctantly, our worlds merged and I took as much, maybe even more than I gave to him. As often as not it was his fields that filled my landscape and beyond that, memories that were clearly not mine, like the part he had played in the war for independence, came to reside in my memory. I imagined myself racing, as he had done, across the green to the big tree and standing there trembling, looking down towards the low road to the town. I was there, taking part, learning to look back in the same way as he did and learning to see what he saw.

By the end of the winter I had developed ways of avoiding those conversations with my father. But I did not stop thinking or talking about going home. That was something we all did, believing we could go any time we wanted to. None of us said so, it was too definite for that. Going home stood at the centre of everything and was, for the first few months or so, accepted as the most important consideration any time a new step into life in England had to be taken. The bigger that step the more we talked about going home. Lil could not understand this. She couldn't see why Bríd was reluctant to enter into hire purchase schemes or join the Christmas club at the Co-op.

Each time she came down to our flat she left with the same expression of disbelief. Her face became fixed in a triangular shape with her eyebrows rising up to meet each other in the middle of her forehead. When she left Bríd always said the same thing,

'What's the point when we might find ourselves at home this side of Christmas.'

Holding on firmly to the belief that we were always just about to pack our bags and leave, we tiptoed into life in England, never missing an opportunity to impress on each other that we belonged elsewhere.

I did not get a school uniform until a letter arrived from the social worker. There was an X marked in the margin beside the part where it said that financial help was available to those parents who could not comply with the school rules on dress. Bríd was quick to tell me that even though I would be getting a uniform, without financial help, it would probably be a waste of money. 'If we decide to go home,' she said looking at me, 'then you would only get a few weeks' wear out of it. Very annoying.' And she looked reassuringly annoyed.

She went to great lengths all through those first months to protect us and, I suppose, herself from the grim fact that there was no choice. We were staying indefinitely. If that fact ever threatened to break through the defences she created, then more extreme steps were immediately taken to make sure that it did not succeed. I can't remember the precise details which led her to pack the tan suitcase and the Travelight one afternoon just before Christmas. We were well on our way to Euston Station before she would answer any of the questions I was asking her. She kept on saying that we had to hurry, that she would explain what was happening when she got a minute. I was so willing to be convinced that when she told us we were on our way home I believed her. And maybe for that moment we were actually going. But I could not ignore the light-hearted desperation that laced her excitement, jumping from one concern to the next, plans to buy presents for people at home, the stain on her coat, the look on Babs' face and the endless arranging of the tan suitcase and the Travelight. Then, almost as if it was a strategy she had worked out in advance, she carefully introduced the first minor drawbacks to the plan by fixing on something she forgot to say to my father. This oversight became more and more important until we began to get anxious about going. By the time we were in Euston we were ready to be defeated by the slightest setback. Eventually, at the precarious moment when we actually turned to go back there was the muted fear that we might be found out telling lies to each other, not only about our trip to Euston but about our future. Still, Bríd seemed to be a little bit ahead all the time, in control of everything that was happening.

When we arrived back in the flat there was no sense of disappointment. We were elated by the plan to postpone the trip until the end of the following week or sometime towards the end of the month – or as soon as the school holidays started. We told each other how easy it was just to get on the train in Euston at nine o'clock and arrive home by lunchtime the following day. It wasn't even all that expensive and we could stay with Queenie for the first few nights and then when our own house was properly aired we could move in there.

The belief that our real life was taking place elsewhere drew us together. It was a sort of conspiracy in which we had all become involved and I was more than content to play my part. We were, I think, inclined to see ourselves as long-term tourists and every Sunday during that first year we went to visit the sights. We would stand in front of the Houses of Parliament, Big Ben, Buckingham Palace, imagining the responses of all the people we knew at home. Babs, Queenie and Joan Mackey may as well have been standing there with us because every detail of their response was conjured up by Bríd. For me it was Hegarty and I roared a description of his face into Bríd's ear as the rollercoaster in Battersea Funfair plunged to what felt like certain doom. I whispered a similar description in Madame Tussaud's. I imagined his expression when at the end of the summer term, I won the one hundred yards sprint at the school sports. I watched him grow silent as I gave demonstrations of my walkie-talkie, my Diskette and my transistor radio.

Our biggest concern, as we settled in, was that the life we were building in England would somehow come to replace all that had gone before. No matter how many ways we had of telling each other that it would not, the possibility that it might did not go away. Sometimes it was as if my father was just sitting there waiting for one of us to do something, say something, use an expression or a gesture we had learned at school and so show our willingness to take on the manners of the world about us. It would all have been much easier if he had been able to say something directly. But his way was to withdraw slowly, so slowly, most times, that nobody was aware of what he was doing until his silence had turned to hostility. Even then, my sisters often remained unaware of how tense things had become in the flat and so they ran about and laughed and chatted and fought. By the time they understood the sort of things that aggravated him they had become unable, or unwilling, to hide the fact that they were whole-heartedly entering into life in England.

Just before Christmas, as we were getting ready for the Club concert, Gretta and Agnes were mimicking their Irish dancing and singing teacher. Their voices, shrill and screeching, vied with each other at the highest reaches of our own national anthem. They had been practising it every Sunday for weeks because singing it at the end of the concert was one of the high points of the night. I could feel my father's rage mount and I was frightened, too frightened to look over towards the corner where he was sitting reading the paper. But when Gretta, determined to be the loudest, began to make retching noises between the words of the song, I was unable to stop myself. At that precise moment his anger broke, shooting across the room like a fissure across ice and in its trail my father, stampeding, unstoppable, blind with rage. Gretta was still laughing when she fell to the ground, unsure of what had happened. And even after a minute or so, still not fully convinced that she had fallen because my father had hit her across the side of her head with such unrestrained force that it seemed like part of something outside of himself. I thought she would cry or get hysterical like she did on the day Queenie would not let her sit at the table with us. But she just put her hand over her ear and held it there while she tried to contain what looked like her determination to get revenge. My father went back to his chair and held his newspaper high up in front of his face. She sat on the ground for a little while and then very quietly began to move nearer and nearer to where he was sitting. When she was only inches away from his newspaper she started to pull faces, gargoyle-like contortions, made with straining noises that he must have heard. Agnes and I were unnerved by her recklessness and tried to beckon her to stop. But she got more reckless and pushed her face right up to the newspaper which, without warning, folded so fast that she fell backwards. My father stepped over her and walked past us on his way out, before we had arrived any-where near the level of fear towards which we were travelling.

It was a victory, even though it did not seem like that at the time because Gretta broke into a fit of compulsive crying. All the way through the concert that night she was drawing in rapid short breaths as if she might burst into tears again. But at the end of the concert she remained silent during the national anthem.

There were other victories. Lots of them and not all so hard won. They happened gradually, the outcome of just being there, ordinary day to day things that could not be challenged. And my father grew weary of trying to stop us behaving as if we belonged. The odds were against him because things that made our position seem less temporary happened one after another and often as a result of each other. The most important of these was Bríd's job.

When we had been there a little under a year she began working as a cashier in a butcher's shop on the High Street. She sat in a sort of glass box from eight until one every day except Sunday. It had been Lil's job for years – until she got a job as a manageress of a launderette. The butcher's shop and the launderette were next door to each other and every morning Bríd and Lil left together, all dressed up and full of purpose. We were usually at school when she got back and on Saturdays I was nearly always out doing something. But when we got in she told us all the things the butchers said. These men, Nick, Bert and Mr Rupton, the head butcher, took their places among us like cardboard cutouts in a play theatre. Lil, who knew everything about them, released details of their lives beyond the butcher's shop, not all at once, but measured out as though the information was part of the job and she was teaching my mother the ropes. Bríd listened eagerly, her eyes darting in my direction whenever Lil lowered her voice to tell her something she did not want us to hear. But even so there was still a sense in which she never entered fully into life in England.

It is difficult to pinpoint exactly when or how this became apparent. The moments were so slight as to be almost imperceptible; moments when she seemed to stand somewhere between the facts of everyday life and the fiction she created to keep us from having to accept ourselves as belonging. I stood beside her in the Co-op once, afraid of what was being revealed as she repeated in a slow, drawn out way something the sales assistant at the fruit and vegetable counter had said.

'What with the weekend coming most of the perishables will probably be reduced.'

Bríd stared vacantly at some blackish bananas. The lady

tried to fill the moment with more information.

'Not by much, mind you, it's frowned on by the regional manager, but we do it anyway, bring down the price, just enough to make sure they're bought. Otherwise they'd perish at the weekend, more so than during the week, odd isn't it?'

The woman's expression changed as she began to sense that Bríd was not examining the bananas at all. I thought she was going to stop speaking altogether but she quickly gathered pace again and charging her voice with a new sense of urgency told us more about what happens to the vegetables at the weekend.

'Sometimes I come in here on a Monday morning and I know right well that the cauliflowers have started to rot even though they have been in the cold room where the fruit and veg are kept at night and at the weekends, the perishables, not everything.'

Bríd walked away.

The woman stopped mid-sentence, smiled vaguely in my direction and said, 'Takes all sorts don't it?'

When I caught up with Bríd she was no different than usual, but as we were crossing the street she asked me if I knew whether or not my father had put oil on the gate hinge. She emphasized each word as though the question she was asking was very important. I could have said I didn't know straight away. But I held back, hoping that by treating the question with the same seriousness as she had asked it, I could grasp what was going on.

My answer was as considered as I could make it but it did not bring me any nearer to her. I wasn't even sure, for a moment or two, that she heard me because she followed with something even more unexpected than her question about the oil.

'If I had gone about it the right way I'd have had a list, it is easy to forget about the small things like the gate. Then they have to wait another year.'

Bríd had no stories about the past. No part of the world we left was, for her, in any way wrapped up and put away and so it remained totally alive, coursing around and then crowding in whenever she was overwhelmed by the way things were or just off guard.

The evening Kennedy was assassinated, about two months after we arrived, Lil burst into the flat and told us to turn on our television. She did not say why but just stood there looking at the set with her hands covering all of her face except for one eye. There were long pauses as the announcer tried to make sense of what was going on and during these pauses Lil repeated what he had said. When the first news bulletin was over she made a list of people she would have to ring. It was as if a close relative was dying. All this time Bríd was standing in the doorway, drying her hands very slowly and smiling in disbelief. There was nothing unusual about that, she often smiled when she was unsure of what was going on. But when she began to laugh we all looked at each other hoping that she might stop and at the same time wondering what we ought to do.

Her laugh got louder and more frightening, as if some great secret she had been harbouring had been disclosed, or as if something she believed in had been shown up as a great sham. Lil and my father glanced at each other, each trying to gauge if the other was going to do something. When it became clear to Lil that my father wasn't, she walked over to where Bríd stood with her head thrown back in laughter.

Lil told us to leave the room and from behind the bedroom door we heard her trying to restrain Bríd as she accused my father of everything, including – indirectly – the death of Kennedy, which by that stage had been declared as certain.

He did not reply, or if he did we did not hear him. Then the occasional break came, intervals that gradually got longer until it became clear that whatever was happening was playing itself out. But I knew that it was still not safe to leave the bedroom.

Lil left and as soon as the door closed Bríd started to speak again. This time her voice was calm, resigned.

'We are here to stay. That's the sum of it.'

She had said what she never let any of us even think, let alone say. He was slow to reply.

'Well, the house is still there, I'm not stopping you, just as I didn't stop you coming.'

I sat on the bedroom floor near the door, imagining that there was an answer to what he had said. But each time I came close to it I found myself moving back until I was suddenly forced, by what I heard Bríd say, to confront it head on.

'We can't go back to living from hand to mouth, like tinkers.'

I scraped the mustard-coloured lino with my nail. Underneath there was a layer of black oily rubber which I tried to scrape, remembering, in snatches, the way the day at the castle ended with the sound of swarming crows.

When we were eventually called out by Bríd I was all prepared to pick my steps carefully but she made it clear straight away that she did not want to be treated any differently than usual. It was over.

But it was more than over, if that's possible, because almost immediately afterwards it seemed as though it had never happened. Nothing changed at all. We were still just about to leave at any moment. But whenever I try to piece together the events of that first winter, or even of the first few years, that evening emerges as the memory around which all memories of the early years in England gather.

Months, even years disappear into the routine. It has a colourless undefined quality, one long bus journey, the supermarket, trolleys full of food, plates of jelly and custard on the low table in front of our big television, Lil coming and going and the Club every Sunday. But there was always something to look forward to, even things like watching Opportunity Knocks, with the light switched off and the low table in front of the TV covered with opened packets of biscuits. Afterwards we talked about it, laughing at the people who thought they were talented. And Gretta mimicked them, twisting about and singing with a nasal drawl until Bríd told her the wind might change. At times like that, leaving seemed very far away. But the plan to return had only been edged to the side. That's all. And when our first trip home became definite the plan was once more at the centre of things. We saw the trip as a sort of trial run for the day we would leave permanently. Tickets were bought. Letters were sent. Letters arrived. There was not a minute to spare.

7

We had been there two and a half years and if we had been able to take stock we would have accepted that, like lots of people we knew, we were going home on holiday. But even though we were only going home for a week the word holiday was not mentioned.

Out of the blue, on the way back from the Saint Patrick's Day celebration at the Club, my father announced that we would be going home within the month. He had never announced anything before, at least not like that. He rarely spoke in full sentences and if what he said drew too much attention then he quickly played it down. That was how I had come to see him and I never imagined that anything could bring about so startling a change in him.

He had kept it all secret for a long time and from the way he spoke to Bríd when we got home, I gathered she knew nothing about it either. She listened, wide-eyed, as he told her about an invitation to the Fiftieth Anniversary of the 1916

Rebellion. Then she began to complain, but only half-heartedly. I think she wanted to congratulate him without changing the way they usually spoke to each other.

'You must have known this for a while. You surely wouldn't have been asked at this stage, expecting you to drop everything and go.'

'I got the letter a while ago all right. From Fonsie Dineen.'

'When?'

'Back a while ago, near the end of January.'

'That's nearly two months ago.'

'That long, is it?' He spoke slowly as if he had just made the connection. 'I thought,' and he stopped to think, 'I thought it might all come to nothing so I said nothing. It was the best thing to say nothing.'

Bríd went around the room straightening things, going on as if the conversation was all just by the way. I tried to be casual, wondering what she would say if she spoke again.

'What of it anyway, it makes no difference now.' Then, almost as though she regretted the sharpness of her reply, she added – full of enthusiasm, 'I'll write to Queenie straight away.'

'We shouldn't have to stay with Queenie for more than a night or two.'

His pace quickened. 'If I can get a fire going in the kitchen as soon as we get there the house should be well aired by the following day. Be sure and mention to her that we'll be moving down after a day or so.'

'I will.' She spoke quietly. Her voice sounded different, curious, patient and at the same time full of interest.

'What on earth made you think that it might all have come to nothing. Was it something that was said in the letter?'

'No. Yes, in a roundabout way, I have the letter here if you want to read it.'

From his back pocket my father took out a heavily creased envelope.

Bríd looked at it for a great deal longer than it took to read it, she seemed to come to the bottom of the page several times before she handed it to me. She said nothing at first. She just beamed – so full of pride that I kept looking up from the letter, trying to make a connection between her excitement and what I was reading.

'Why didn't you say anything about the medal? You said nothing about the medal.'

'It still might come to nothing, that's the point.' His voice was high, excitable. 'I wasn't in the Rising. Nobody around our part was. Anyway, in 1916 I was no more than nine or ten.'

I wondered if my view of his past was all wrong. I tried to remember what I knew about him before we came to England and what he had told me since. I tried to remember precisely what he said he did in the war for independence. But that unexpected glimpse I got of him from the train on the Sunday morning we arrived in England became fixed in my mind. All attempts I made to form a picture of his life before that failed. It was impossible to imagine that the person standing on the platform had, on the night of the big fire, stood behind the tree in the middle of the green watching the low road to the town. I remembered him telling me, more than once, that it was the best lookout spot in the whole area.

'What about the big fire?'

I had spoken without intending to and they both looked at me in such a way that I began to feel that my question was foolish. But my father's voice, soft and at the same time full of seriousness, filled me with a peculiar sense of my own importance and I quickly lost track of my train of thought.

'Well, the big fire was in December 1922, that was after the War of Independence but it was still part of it in a way.'

I nodded, pretending that it had all become clear but he must have sensed that I hadn't pieced it together fully because when he replied he spoke slowly as if he was about to explain it all from the beginning.

'What they'll be commemorating when we go home is the 1916 Rising. I don't see how they would want to give a medal to someone who wasn't there.'

Bríd smiled and then in a great fluster of impatience told him that there was no difference between what was going on in 1916 and 1922. 'It was,' she said with great authority, 'all part of the same fight for independence and that's why they are giving you the medal.'

My father smiled.

On the following Saturday morning we went to Balham and in a wave of great excitement, and endless speculation about what would be suitable for the presentation ceremony, we all got new outfits. Swayed by the talk about the freedom medal and the commemorations, my father peeled notes off a wad as thick as his wrist. I got a Beatle suit and Beatle boots. Our bags took up a full extra seat on the bus on the way home. Bríd sat in the seat behind guarding them, more delighted with what was happening than I had ever seen her before.

When everything was going well in our family the whole pace quickened. It had a ragtime tempo to it. At times like this, Gretta led the way, finishing people's sentences at high speed, filling in the gaps, repeating things people said, laughing, running away. She was like a cheerleader, full of belief, making 'what if' type suggestions and 'then what if' and so on. One of her specialities was reading things out loud, directions, advertisements. Anything. She flitted about the place half-dancing, half-gliding, making up tunes to accompany her unpredictable steps and often knocking things down. Her eyes would almost pop when she laughed and she laughed a lot, which is probably one of the reasons why people did not get annoyed when she interrupted their conversation. She even interrupted herself at times, telling us things in a high-pitched voice – against a background of babble and chat which she herself went on providing.

That evening when we got back from Balham we were all practically dancing around the flat. Right at the very centre was Gretta, co-ordinating every twist and turn the excitement took.

To try and calm her down a bit Bríd turned on the television. Within seconds Gretta was leaping up and down chanting, 'Telly's on the blink, telly's on the blink. Hey, look, telly's on the blink.' We all sat watching. A notice appeared apologizing for the interruptions. Her face brimmed with the words before she read them aloud. She read and re-read and kept on re-reading until the programme reappeared. When the flickering started again after a minute or so she began to go through the same routine. When the delay went on she read out the individual words of the apology in a singsong voice. Then when the programme came back on she breathed a great sigh of relief and, slumping back into her chair, said, 'Phew. I'm glad that's over.'

Nobody tried to contain her the way they usually did. My father sat watching television with a broad smile on his face. We kept glancing at him to see how long it was going to last. Agnes quietly went into the bedroom every few minutes to look at the new clothes she got in Balham that afternoon. Later on she reached a point where she could not bear to be parted from them so she brought them out and sat with them on her lap. Bríd went along with it all, floating one moment and spinning the next as Gretta blazed past her at cartoon speed.

There was no let-up in the pace during the days that followed. If anything, the excitement intensified as we tumbled headlong towards the day we were to leave for home.

All the packing was done in advance so when the day eventually came there was little to do but wait. Several times Bríd phoned the dry cleaners, trying to make sure that Gretta's and Agnes's Irish dancing costumes would be ready on time. Gretta had won a few big competitions, not just at the Club. Bríd, hearing from Queenie that there would be a dancing competition during the commemoration ceremonies, decided that Gretta and Agnes would take part. After a lot of plans and counter plans we settled on getting a taxi to the station so we could stop at the dry cleaners on the way. Each new arrangement was made with a concern for detail that brought us to the edge of argument and then immediately back full circle to total agreement. All differences of opinion were swept aside as laughable misunderstandings. The flat became like a transit depot, fully given over to the great business of the day.

The dancing costumes were spread on top of our luggage in their cellophane wrappers, their resplendent colours, luminous green, royal blue, flaming red and yellow, loudly stating our loyalty to all we were about to reclaim. The journey, six hours on the train, four on the boat and then a further two on the train, had all the swing and pace of a marching band. If a drum beat had sounded when, in the early morning, the coastline came into view, none of us would have said anything. It would not have seemed at all strange.

Somewhere behind us England disappeared and with it the previous two and a half years. I began to feel light, full of coarse energy and ready to disregard everything. It was April. Sudden winds swept the deck, dying down as instantly as they blew up. In the lulls there was an almost palpable warmth in the air. I peered in the direction of the coastline as if I was seeing it for the first time. I stretched my arms out as all the new-found energy welling inside me extended from my fingertips to that faraway horizon, the rim of the earth, and back.

At last the train arrived in what we had, all morning, been calling our station. It was very near the town but so different to any of the buildings in the town that it always looked isolated. We were the only ones to get off the train that afternoon and as we grouped loosely around our luggage, looking out for someone we knew, the place seemed more desolate than ever. There was something disappointing about the way the train shunted out of the station. It was, I suppose, the thought that there were other places to go, making our destination seem just one of many. The event was somehow diminished, and the marching band turned into a small family group pushing three tan suitcases along an empty platform.

I tried to will myself back into the whirl of expectation. But, as I backed away, my other memories of the station poured in. I trailed unwillingly in the wake of those memories, seeing my father on his way back to England – sitting in the front seat of the hackney car leaning forward. His knuckles, always pressed white against the dashboard, while he stared out into the distance where the hedges looped over the road. All that time standing on the platform, and maybe it was only a couple of seconds, I tried to hold out against the thought that no matter how many times or under what circumstances I might arrive in that station the feeling would always be one of defeat.

I rose and sank in quick succession, following ideas and thoughts only to let go of them in the same breath. It was a brittle sort of excitement, the sort that brings very small children to the point of laughter just as quickly as it brings them to tears. In an effort to hold onto everything I succeeded in holding onto nothing and only began to feel settled when my father said that he thought he heard a car. I welcomed the chance to focus my attention. Very consciously I framed my expression into the most alert shape I could manage and with my head tilted to one side listened to the hackney car tearing down the station road.

Leaving the engine running, the hackney man rushed onto the platform. When he saw us he slapped his forehead and held his expression of surprise until our smiles broke into laughter. The way he said 'Jesus' was in itself welcoming.

75

Every time he went to speak he said it again. Eventually he followed through with a garbled explanation as to why he had not been there to meet the train. He said he couldn't remember ever being late for the afternoon train before. And on the very day we were on it, if only he had known we were going to be on it, Jesus. We listened to everything he had to say, delighted to be listening, hearing only the sound of the words and the rhythm, all the time smiling as though we were listening to music we knew so well that the pleasure of listening to it lay more in anticipating each phrase than actually hearing it. But he was familiar in other ways too. He had taken his place in the stories and incidents that made up my father's world. He had become the greatest of hackney men, the one who had survived, the one who got all the business, because he was the best. But while my father handed out that kind of title to nearly all the people who played a part in the world he had so reluctantly left, the hackney man almost lived up to the description. Down through the years several other people had gone into the same business. They had, for the most part, come home from England. Their cars with yellow registration plates and peculiar registration numbers were usually much plusher than the hackney man's car. Everyone hired them once and then went back to the original hackney man. I think it must have been the way he entered into things. If he was bringing people to a match he would arrive with the car draped in flags and banners. He would begin hooting long before he came into sight and then roar and shout out the window as he approached. When he was bringing people to a dance he leapt out of the car at the collection point and did a sort of rumba. Whatever the event, it started when he arrived. That included funerals. He wept from the moment the mourners got into the car.

He loaded our suitcases into the boot and in a very short time he was talking to us as though we had never been away. He did not ask the question that was to plague us during the week that followed: How long are you home for? Instead, he told us about all the Rising celebrations and stopped outside the parochial hall to let us see the big outdoor stage they were building for the occasion. It stretched from the top of the parochial hall steps right out and on to the street. Anyone standing towards the front of the stage would have full command of the square it overlooked. To the right of the hall there was a big marquee. Once he had told us about all the details taken into account when the plans were being made for the celebrations, he started the car again. But then with a sudden violent movement he turned to my father who was sitting in the passenger seat.

'Jesus, you'll be, I forgot, you'll be up there, aren't you supposed to be getting one of the medals.'

We were sitting in the back, smiling, edging forward a little, waiting for him to continue.

He began by listing the feats of my father's generation, saying how magnificent they were, picking his words as if he was addressing a public gathering. Before long we were looking solemnly at those great years when the whole nation was on the march to freedom. Everything around us in the town that afternoon, the stage, the bunting, the marquee and the tricolours that hung from the windows, seemed to point back to a more important era than the world to which I thought we were returning. So, when about ten minutes later we drove up outside our house and I stepped out of the hackney car, I felt caged in that past, unable to break loose, rush headlong and grasp the world I came to reclaim.

I tried to move away from the car and follow Bríd who was walking at a rapid pace towards our gate but I was overcome by the sort of fear that sometimes overcame me when, back in London, I was crossing the High Street down at the intersection. I could not move. All I could do was stand there, watching as she made her way down the path to the door of our house. With each step she grew less familiar until she stood in front of the broken door looking like the film star she had become in England. Her hair waved back from her forehead and caught the light so that everything around her softened and blurred. Even the way she stood, holding one side of her coat collar against her cheek, made her glamorous and the house derelict. I twisted the heel of my Beatle boot into the gravel, turning it with fierce concentration, trying above all else not to cry. In spite of my efforts I lost the battle. But it was not sadness that made me cry. It was nothing as drawn out as that, it felt more like anger. And there was the continuous distraction of scents and smells, leading back to things I had not thought about since we left.

Bríd tried to go into the house but the door would not open. We learned later that it had been boarded up from the inside. She called my father who had gone across to Moratorium Row. He gestured to us to go on up to Queenie's and then, raising his chin and speaking loudly, said he would follow us up later. He stood before two old men who were sitting on the wall. They greeted him in an offhand way as though he had been gone for only a few minutes. Plonked on the wall beside these men were two large bulky objects covered with black plastic and tied in two or three places with yellow baling twine. Behind these objects, which were about the same size as the men themselves, was a low scaffold with two planks thrown roughly on top of it.

Bríd thanked the hackney man for stopping to let us look at the house.

'It'll take a bit of mending, were you thinking of staying there tonight?'

He looked in the rear view mirror, waiting for her to reply.

'In a day or two, perhaps.' She spoke with her public voice, the one she used in England. It was strained and slow, every word deliberate, individually shaped so that she would be clearly understood. Suddenly it seemed false in a theatrical sort of way. I wanted to shake her, shout at her, tell her that

78

we were back home again now and she didn't have to speak like that. But I just listened while she said vague things about being home as if she had a take-it or leave-it attitude to it all. The possibility that she might have changed in a permanent way crossed my mind. But when we got out of the car at Queenie's she started laughing skittishly – mimicking her own vagueness in the hackney car. She made it clear that she was playing a part not only for the hackney man but for his wife and everyone else he would tell of our arrival. She laughed loudly as she told Queenie, in detail, everything that had happened since we got off the train. She made the smallest of these things appear funny and we laughed, rising and sinking with her, as we had done over the past two and a half years.

8

Queenie's house was totally unchanged. Two brown and cream coloured china dogs guarded either end of the mantelshelf. A series of ornaments in ever-decreasing size led from the dogs to a low squat clock in the centre. Each object, like articles of the occult, had a quality beyond itself. I stood looking at them full of the reverence they commanded.

'You've grown as big as a house. Let me look at you.'

I wanted to touch them. I wanted to take up the small glass globe and shake it until the Virgin inside disappeared in the snowstorm. I wanted to take down the little kangaroo which held the day's date in its paws and the rest of the year's dates in its pouch.

'Canice Hegarty asked when you were coming, he'll hardly recognize you. I don't know how you can see through that fringe.'

I suddenly remembered the Child of Prague and the way it had fallen the day before we left. I swung around and even before I saw it standing there, mended as good as new, I had begun to hold it in some way responsible for our leaving. It too, with its spiteful little face and all its ornate clothes, seemed to possess powers beyond itself. Sullen, wilful powers.

'He said he'd be down around the green if you came in on the four o'clock.'

Bríd was in the hall, pleading with Gretta and Agnes who, from the moment they discovered that they were sleeping with Queenie in her bed, wanted to go back. They were so put out by this that it did not occur to any of us to ask or even think about where Michael, Queenie's husband, was going to sleep. When I heard that I would be sleeping in the kitchen I got the idea that once everyone else was in bed I could make a detailed inspection of the ornaments.

I walked down past the crumbling church wall, running my fingers over the stones and tracing the contours of the crevices, bewildered by the way it all became familiar again. When I saw Hegarty sitting on the embankment in front of our house I stopped and while I looked at him I felt the stone beneath my hand grow cold. There were two people with him but I did not recognize them. Whenever I thought about being home and meeting him for the first time, he was never with other people. I tightened the thong on my duffel bag and glanced across to where my father stood in front of the two old men.

There were no leaves on the tree in the middle of the green but it was not bare in a stark midwinter way. The tiny green tipped buds had broken through and that lank wintery sheen remained only on the trunk and the main limbs. It was as if I had only been away for a very short time; a time that shrank and even occasionally disappeared altogether as I took command of my own world.

Hegarty and the others did not look up until I was a few paces away from them. When I saw his face I stopped, riveted by his appearance. He had a moustache, a wispy moustache which drooped down around his mouth. I smiled, and thought he would smile too or laugh, but he just pointed at the duffel bag.

'I hope there's a few *Playboy*s in that bag.' The others smirked without moving a single facial muscle. 'And a few frenchies.'

Hegarty continued pointing but turned sideways to look at the others. Their smirks soured to leers – again without any apparent movement.

I do not know why I refused to take stock of what was happening. Some stubborn impulse made me stick to plan and try to make it all turn out just as I imagined it would. I opened the duffel bag, quickly pulling the thong to the end of the cords, concentrating on every movement, battling all the time with the feeling that what I was doing was not going to turn out the way I wanted. Still I persisted, unwilling to abandon the excitement with which I had looked forward to meeting Hegarty again. I began to take out one of the boxes, but could not get it to move because it was so tightly wedged against the other. Pressing them close together and slightly bending the edges I forced them out. The one beneath fell and Hegarty, who had been watching in a careless sort of way, picked it up and examined it.

'What is it, some kind of transistor?'

He tossed it to the older of the two, who by this stage I guessed were brothers. He looked at it and handed it back to Hegarty as though it was of no interest whatsoever. Hegarty then put the box up to his ear and with his eyes almost fully shut started to shout.

'Fab 208. R-A-D-I-O L-U-X-E-M-B-U-R-G. This is B-A-T-T-L-E O-F T-H-E G-I-A-N-T-S and your host all the way from London ... '

He threw the box to me.

'Come on, open the fucken thing – would you.'

I tore the top of the box off.

'It's a walkie-talkie, the other half is here.'

I picked up the other box and took out the cream, book shaped apparatus. When I turned the perspex dial on the side it hissed and crackled.

'What the fuck do you want a walkie-talkie for?'

I was so thrown by Hegarty's question that I gave little or no thought to my reply.

'Well if, if you were at the far side of the moor, over there at the birch trees and you wanted to get in contact with someone, say who was here where we are, you know in a war game or something like that, just . . . '

I did not need to look at them to know that I was losing ground so fast that climbing back would be almost impossible. For a second I considered saying I was only joking. But the two brothers were openly sniggering and I was afraid that anything I said might leave me even more on the outside of things than I already was.

'Tell us,' Hegarty said. 'Who are you with, the Englanders or the Gerries, or are you some kind of fucken Indian chief? Big Chief Mahogany Gas Pipe.'

I tried to hold back the anger I felt.

Hegarty took one of the walkie-talkies, stood up, and holding it like a microphone started shouting into it.

'Hitler,' then much louder. 'Hitler, can you hear me? This is His Divine Majesty the King of England.'

The brothers guffawed, glancing in my direction to see if I was going to do anything to stop Hegarty. I laughed, pretending that I found the whole thing as funny as they did. Hegarty turned the perspex dial as fast as he could. It went around and around until it reached a point beyond which it would not go. He looked at it for a moment and then gripped it firmly and forced it further. When it broke off he let on to be completely surprised.

'This is a heap of Japanese shite.'

He threw it in my direction.

'It never worked anyway.' I said. 'All it did was make that noise.'

That was true. When I brought it up to Clapham Common all it did was buzz and hiss. But no matter how hard I tried to convince myself that the set never worked, the belief that it would once I got home, remained. I had blamed interference from traffic and all sorts of other interference in London for making it hiss and crackle. My father had agreed with this whole-heartedly and so for two years it had sat on top of the wardrobe in the bedroom, packed and ready for our return. It had not occurred to me to change the plan.

My father walked away from the old men and over towards us. He asked the brothers who they were and followed through with questions about the townsland they came from. I heard their cautious replies as I tried to think of ways of changing the direction in which things were going between me and Hegarty. If I went back to Queenie's and got the Diskette and some records I might make a better impression but I had a vague inkling that making a better impression might not be the way to undo what had happened. And then, just as I was beginning to contain the devastation I felt, my father picked up the broken walkie-talkie and it all began again.

I listened reluctantly as he slowly described the shop, one of the biggest toy shops in London, where we bought it. I was forced to remember the day, shortly before our first Christmas in London, when we all went to Oxford Street. We tried to walk together but kept on bunching in on one another, breaking up and then re-forming until we eventually gave up and just tried to keep sight of each other.

The shop was huge. Everything in it glistened. Two broad staircases, one on each side of the ground floor emporium, curved up to the second floor which overlooked the vast display of toys in front of us. From the way Bríd and my father smiled at each other, I sensed that they considered just

84

being there an achievement. I must have seen the big glass booths, plonked half-way up each stairway, but they did not register because I was so overwhelmed by seeing so much at once. Not until Bríd pointed to the banner, saying 'Walkie-Talkie Demonstration Booths', did I actually grasp what they were. Immediately I wanted to have a go. Bríd persuaded my father to join the queue leading up the stairs to the booth on the right and waited with Gretta and Agnes while I queued for the one nearest to us.

Once inside our booths, my father waved over to me. He held the walkie-talkie like a prayer book, inspecting it from a distance as if he did not expect it to work. In between the crackling and the high-pitched piercing squeaks I heard his voice but the voice I replied to was Hegarty's.

'Position?'

'Silver birch coral.'

'Over and Out?'

'Right ... Ready for combat?'

'Over and Out.'

My father began to examine the broken perspex dial carefully. Held between his stumpy forefinger and his thumb it looked frail and useless. I was determined not to be there when he asked the question so I jumped up and went over to the house.

Shortly after we went to England the house had been rented by a hairdresser. Dineen did not tell us at the time and when Queenie had asked him what steps should be taken to have the rent sent to us he told her that it hardly covered his expenses and not to mention the matter if she was writing. So we did not hear about it until the final plans for going home were being made. By that time the hairdresser had left and a new tenant had not been found. I knew for certain that Bríd thought Dineen had been high-handed. Her answers to the questions I asked about it were vague and she seemed relieved when my father brought the conversation to a close by saying that we would have heard from Dineen if he had collected rent on our behalf.

My father had known Dineen all his life. They had been at school together and my father felt personally involved in Dineen's success. He was chairman of the commemoration committee and I think we all felt that not only had he played a big part in bringing about our return home, but that he had made the whole episode seem triumphant. Then, just before we left London, a letter had arrived from Dineen addressed to the whole family, announcing that on the day of the commemoration ceremony, he and a surprise dignitary, who was going to present the medals, would personally collect us and bring us to the parochial hall. My father made no effort to hide his satisfaction. He was full of praise for Dineen and listed all his merits, one after another until they formed a sort of barrier, shutting out any questions about him which might have lingered. Those questions did not surface again, except maybe in a very undefined way, until I stood in front of the window of our house trying to make out what it was like inside.

I was only able to see a small part of the floor because the hairdresser's three wigged heads filled the lower part of the window. There was something eerie about being so close to them. One of the wigs had slipped to the side making the model look distraught, even a bit deranged. Above them was a sign listing the times the salon was open and the different types of hairstyle on offer. The lettering had faded to yellow except for the bit which read 'beehives, bouffants and permanents'. That part was handwritten and had lots of twirls and flourishes.

I was so intent on trying to see inside that I did not hear my father coming until he was right behind me. I stood back and pointed to the small gap through which I had been looking. He cupped his hands around his eyes and, bending down a little, moved right up to the glass. Without saying a word to me or Hegarty, who had just made his way over, he went up to the front door. When he discovered that it had been boarded up from the inside he began to shake it and then jostle it until he forced a space big enough to get his arm through. Within seconds he wrenched the boards away from the door surround and broke through. I expected him to turn around and say something but he charged ahead and although we followed almost immediately, he was already pulling one of the three sinks from the wall when we arrived at the kitchen door.

Hegarty laughed when he saw what was going on and straight away wedged an old board in behind some of the water pipes and started levering them away from the wall. He carried on as if it was all a big joke, unaware that the strength with which my father was tugging the sink from its fittings came from wild anger. I watched him grip the sink so tightly that his hands quivered. When it came away, like a big deep-rooted molar, pipes burst and rust-coloured water shot across the room. Hegarty hopped from foot to foot with excitement until my father, rushing out to the water mains, pushed him out of the way. Even then he did not realize the way things were going because when he regained his balance he picked up one of the pipes and sprayed the room with rusty water. Holding his thumb over part of the pipe he managed to direct a single jet of water over at the wigged heads. He yelped as he displaced each in turn, making swooching sounds as he created great fans of water, stretching from one side of the room to the other. The flow eased and quickly ebbed to a dribble. I left to go upstairs not only, or even mainly, because I did not want to be there when my father came back in, but out of confusion. The scale of the house was different. Everything I saw or touched clashed with the memory I had of it. The stairwell shrank around me and the steps folded in on each other, making the climb to the landing possible in what felt like a single leap. I almost lost my balance in my own room when I found I could rest my hand on the bed while still standing at the door. But before I could adjust to the new dimensions of the place, I was rooted to the spot by the sight of thousands of dead bees on the floor. I was, from the instant I saw them, fully aware that they were dead but some primitive impulse whispered caution. I heard myself say the word 'dead' in a long drawn out way, hoping the word would last until I reached the window and at the same time squirming as their crispy frames crackled under my feet.

To my surprise, everything from the window – my window on the world – appeared in harmony. The green, webbed by the widely splayed shadows of the big tree, was still. And when Hegarty walked down the path below me he just took his place in the quiet order of things. Everything he had done that afternoon lost its edge. I stood and looked across the moor to the point where the tufts that pocked the burnished grass grew pencil-line thin. I did not want to think about anything definite in case those thoughts displaced the feeling of being home. I stayed there for a long time, long after my father had left, and then eventually went back up to Queenie's.

Bríd answered the door.

'Michael's dead. He died nearly two years ago. Don't mention it.'

As we walked into the kitchen, Queenie looked up from the magazine she was reading. She had a vacant way of staring that sometimes gave the impression she was frightened.

Michael, her husband, was often described by her as 'not strong'. As long as I could remember she talked about his death as if it was just about to happen. So the news was not in itself shocking. But I was initially very put out by the thought that something as serious as that could have happened without us hearing about it. But this too was in keeping with the sort of person Michael was. He did everything he could to avoid being noticed. I never heard him speak. Once, when the County Council for which he worked was repairing the path near the school, I said hello to him. He did not answer so I said hello again. No response. At first I felt invisible but afterwards came around to the belief that it was he who felt invisible. He spent most of the time with the old men over at Moratorium Row and because they were all so alike in appearance I could not, as Bríd spoke about him, form a distinct picture of him. A cap, bicycle clips, greyish-brownish clothes, a pioneer pin. That was Michael, a collection of things. After his death, Queenie laid these things out on a bench in a shed behind the house and lurking around that bench was a sense of his presence, no different to that which surrounded him when he was alive.

Queenie spent most of that first afternoon telling Bríd about Michael's death. That evening, when Queenie was out at Devotions, Bríd explained to us that Michael's death and the ordeal that followed had been so terrible for Queenie that she had been unable to speak about it for over a year.

He had had a heart attack on a Sunday morning in early August and died instantly. The doctor from the town was on holiday and the young locum was called. Queenie, who – in her mind – had lived through the moment many times, had worked out a plan based on sketchy knowledge of what happens when a person dies. Her great fear was that rigor mortis would set in and his mouth would be frozen open for the wake. To avoid this she opened his mouth a little and, once she was certain he was dead, put a raw potato in. By pressing his upper and lower teeth into it she managed to shut it so that it would remain shut. When he examined the body, the young locum told Queenie that because Michael had had a raw potato stuffed into his mouth, an official post mortem would have to be carried out. He assured her that it was all routine and so it was. When the town doctor returned a few days later he made a special point of telling Queenie that it was the young locum's lack of experience which made him take the ill-advised step of ordering a post mortem. But on

the Sunday morning of Michael's death the word on everybody's lips was not post mortem but murder.

Bríd and Queenie were very different from each other in
most ways but there were a few similarities which marked
them out as sisters. Bríd's outrage at the notion that Queenie
had murdered Michael was just as I imagined Queenie's own
had been when she told Bríd her story earlier that day. She
threw her head back and then, as if she was in pursuit of a
word that would fully enclose all that outrage, she brought
her head forward – darting from side to side like a fish after
its prey. I liked the way they talked to each other. It had a
pace of its own, a bit like a prayer in which the words gave
way to the rhythm. But my father was thinking along different
lines as Bríd described Queenie's ordeal, because when she
finished, he said that if Queenie lived in England she would
have been sent for treatment and might have ended up in a
mental home. It was a swipe at England and, as such, very
familiar. But Bríd saw it as a swipe at Queenie and said
so much so quickly in Queenie's defence that there was no
possibility of telling her she had misunderstood him. That
was just the beginning. Days of glances followed. Curt replies,
things asked for with crispy politeness and endless pin-stab-
bing gibes – Bríd defending Queenie against the world and in
particular, my father. It would have been understandable if he
had been critical of Queenie. But he was not and so I came to
see Bríd as the source of the tetchy atmosphere that made
even the most ordinary everyday dealings we had with each
other seem brittle. At the time it seemed to be a straightforward division, with Bríd and Queenie comfortably on one
side and the rest of us uncomfortably on the other. I was
reluctant to take into account that Bríd had spent all of her
single life with Queenie. And after she got married they still
spent a lot of time together, a great deal more than Bríd had
spent with my father. The way they were constantly part of
each other's lives, endlessly in and out of each other's houses,

led to an ease between them that was often missing between my father and Brid. She would not have admitted this. She wouldn't even have thought about it, which is probably why a niggling resentment grew against my father. He never defended himself, just remained silent, went for walks all the time. Those walks were exactly like the ones he used to go on when he came home before. He would start out with a sense of purpose, as if he was going somewhere in particular, and would arrive back with an air of defeat about him.

9

There was a peculiar smell from the couch in Queenie's kitchen, a bit like the smell of mutton boiling but with a sourness to it, concentrated around the spot where the orange and brown cushion, my pillow, lay. I could not sleep. The smell was only part of the problem. The couch was too small, but not by much. If I kept my knees a little bent I could just about fit. But I kept thinking about stretching, much more than I usually did, and so I had to think of ways of forgetting how cramped I was. I thought about the events of the day, a day that seemed to have spilled over.

One thought in particular, my father's opinion that Queenie might be regarded as mentally ill in England, kept going around my head. I was tired. I had not slept on the boat the night before and although I did not miss that sleep during the day, a time came in the evening when I could not wait for the others to leave the kitchen so I could go to sleep. By the time they did, my tiredness had gone beyond itself and turned into a mildly delirious form of energy. I lay on the couch in that heightened state, aware of every discomfort and every smell, unable to control the pace at which my thoughts were racing. And so, in a detached way, I watched them crash around, burst into fragments and re-form again. I watched the question about Queenie being mentally ill appear and then disappear. In the half-logic of fatigue I imagined I might be able to find an answer if I could first of all remember the name of the boy I had been told to sit beside on the afternoon of my first day at school in England. He had emerged from nowhere, presenting himself as a clue in the search. Then I became so preoccupied with trying to remember his name that I lost sight of the question about Queenie, vitally important an instant before. I never saw that boy again. He had an Irish name, which is probably why I was told to sit beside him. But that was after the teacher had asked me several questions about my interests. It was a hobbies class that took place on the first Monday in every month. Everyone looked forward to it and they brought in lots of different things, aeroplane assembly kits, stamp albums and approvals, hamsters. One boy was constructing a ship in a bottle and the boy in front had a goldfish in a bowl. When the teacher asked me if I had a hobby I said yes but then I couldn't come up with anything. He kept on naming hobbies and I kept on shaking my head. Then he gave up and told me to sit beside, and I suddenly remembered his name, Walsh. Patrick Walsh. The teacher had said it as he pointed to an empty place beside a boy who looked unfriendly and who immediately warned me that if I called him Patrick trouble would follow.

'My name is Rick, get that? Rick – and I've got a temper, ask anyone.'

He was reading a magazine about his hobby. Mountain climbing. He said it with such ease and authority that I had no difficulty imagining him standing on the top of a high mountain holding the Union Jack. He was an expert. I saw it all written down in his hobby log book. There were pages and pages of details, mountain heights, peaks and slopes of England, Scotland and Wales. Conditions in spring, summer, autumn and winter. And the list, or lists, of gear; fell boots, double-insole socks, reinforced laces, knee pads. The equipment he already had was underlined in heavy black pen and the equipment he hoped to get was underlined in heavy blue pen. He told me that he intended climbing three years later, when he reached the permitted age, fifteen. Until then he had to remain an associate member of the mountaineering club and was restricted to hill walking. He had done some hill walking the previous summer and he told me that he had turned out to be quite good at it. I made no connection between hill walking as Rick described it and walking in the hills as I knew it.

What my father said about Queenie hovered like a kite and tailing behind it were a whole string of memories from those early weeks in England. The most vivid of these was the first swimming class. I did not want to think about it and so I tried to will myself back from the precipice of sleep, where much of what I did not want to think about lurked. But unable to remain awake any longer, I began to lose ground and drift forward. As I got nearer I imagined I saw the swimming instructor.

'Let's have a look then son, best be certain before we begin, up and down, two lengths.'

The class waited at the edge of the pool. I had been given a choice by the instructor. Stroke Improvement or Beginners. I opted for Stroke Improvement and was delighted with the chance, two whole lengths, to show him and the others how good I was.

I wanted to turn back, to look away but I was too tired. Far too tired. And so I tumbled helplessly towards a scene which until then I had somehow managed to forget.

Each swell of water I displaced came rolling back over my

head. In order to keep going I had to scoop up larger and larger sections of the pool, sucking and choking on chlorine. There was a ringing sensation in my head, a dizziness that spun out making increasingly wider circles, going out beyond my head, forming a sort of whirlpool that drew me back, headfirst and then down towards the bottom of the pool. I turned in such a way as to get the side of my mouth just above the water and drew in what air I could before I sank again.

I had stepped over the precipice. I even had the sensation that as I passed by the instructor he had smiled and so I was shocked by the gruff way he called me back and totally terrified when he caught me by the hair and started to drag me in. When I came to, stretched out on the ridged tiles at the side of the pool, I heard him telling the others I would be all right. My limbs were heavy, even moving my fingers felt peculiar. Despite the strained knotted feeling at the back of my neck I sat up.

The whole class was there, staring, some in disbelief and others with expressions of pity. They were relieved when the instructor, sodden after his spectacular rescue dive, gave the go ahead for laughter. 'Where did you learn to swim, son – the Amazon?'

I spat laughter and choked on laughter and sneezed laughter, slipping away behind my performance, out and away, tearing across the moor to the high reeds at the far side of the birch trees. There, kneeling on the mossy tufts, I slowly parted the reeds and peered into the darkness.

I moved my eyes from side to side and around, trying to make out the shapes that throbbed in the fleshy pink light of the Sacred Heart lamp. I could see the outline of the Child of Prague. I kept my eyes fixed on it for a long time, afraid that if I looked away it might move. When I was certain that it would not I began to examine the ornaments on the mantelpiece. Every so often I glanced back suddenly at the Child of Prague, half-expecting to catch it moving. The delft dogs with their brown and gold manes stared across the room in such a fixed way that I checked the far wall to make sure there was nothing unusual. Once the room came fully into focus I was no longer afraid to close my eyes and I quickly fell asleep again.

When I woke, or just before I woke, I had the sensation that there was someone in the room. I hoped it was Bríd. All through the night I felt that she was in danger. I did not know why. I could not remember enough. Only one fragment remained, a moment when she came stumbling out the door of our house ducking and craning as hundreds of bees swarmed around her hair. When she spoke her voice was surprisingly calm. 'You won't get much chance to sleep on in the mornings there.'

That was obvious, but I was so glad to hear Bríd's voice with all its familiar tones that when she spoke I thought only about her and the way everything became normal around her.

I had no plans for the day. Being home was such an event in itself that I didn't bother to work out the details of what I would do each day. Anyway, so much of our time at home was planned around the various commemoration ceremonies that I almost regarded the other days as leading to the first of those events, the opening night of the carnival. The question of plans came up after breakfast when Queenie asked me what I was going to do for the day. I told her I didn't know. But she waited as though she expected me to make up my mind and so I had to think of something. I told her I might call for Hegarty.

'You'll probably find him in all right,' she said 'because he only goes to work half the time' and then turning to Bríd, she added, 'He couldn't care less about losing a day's pay and Babs lets him do whatever he wants for fear he'd take the boat and she'd never see him again.' And then almost under her breath she added 'Just like the father.'

I put on my hipsters, denim shirt and floral tie. And I put

four singles into the side pocket of my Diskette.

I knocked on Hegarty's door and turned towards Moratorium Row. On my way down I had been trying to work out what the two shapes covered with black plastic were. The old men had to sit in between, or on either side of these shapes, and lean out whenever they wanted to speak to each other.

I knocked the door again and swung round. I didn't want to be standing there staring at whoever opened it. I felt certain someone would, even after I had been waiting for about five minutes. Finally the door moved a little, opening slowly until there was a space about the width of a clenched fist, maybe a little more. Thinking that it was stuck I pushed it. It moved a few inches, then back to its original position. Babs' head appeared. That's all, just her head. I stood looking at her and she at me. I was waiting for the door to open before I spoke.

'Look at the size of you – Lord help us.'

I couldn't figure out why she would not open the door further. I couldn't even see her ears. Her face was thin. Two heavy lines ran from underneath her cheek bones right down to the corners of her mouth. Her lips and her chin moved from side to side all the time.

'Look at you.'

I looked down at my hipsters and my Beatle boots.

'Will Canice be out soon?'

I asked the question with little or no interest. I suddenly wanted to be on my own. I wanted to think about why Babs was standing there holding the door as if she did not know me very well.

'He's gone to work, he won't be in 'til after six.'

I didn't believe her. It was all too suspicious.

'I'm going into the town, I might call in on him.'

I expected her to look alarmed but she looked relieved and asked me to wait at the door while she went to get something he had forgotten. Several minutes later she came back, at least her hand came out the narrow opening holding a small parcel wrapped in sliced pan paper.

'His sandwiches. He forgot them. He's always in a hurry. I'm always telling him he'll rush himself into an early grave.'

The door closed at the same slow pace as Babs' hand and face went in and I stood there trying to make sense of what had happened. The whole way into the town, nearly three miles, I kept thinking of ways to make Babs feel sorry for what she had done. I conjured up all sorts of unlikely scenes, starting with me having a big present for her – so big that I had to ask her to open the door a bit wider to let me through. I sauntered along the road, smiling to myself as I spoke to her, stretching my face and opening my mouth in an exaggerated way.

'Not at all. Of course it's for you. Well you nearly didn't get it, I thought you were going to leave me standing at the door.'

I came to tell her something of great importance, that she had won an unthinkably large amount of money. She clasped her hands. The door swung open. With each new announcement, one more fantastic than the next, the door swung open quicker. And then I got fed up. I no longer cared if I ever saw her again.

I put the first single into the Diskette and turned it up to peak volume. I shouted the words, striding along in bouncy leaps, giving everything, every shard of belief and feeling to the music. When I had played 'You've Lost that Lovin' Feeling' five or six times, I changed to 'Twist and Shout' – and safely lost in the wild tearing sounds of the Diskette, I howled at a world where things were growing less precious by the moment.

I sat on the wall that surrounded the tree opposite Hegarty's work. I didn't know what part of the shop he worked in. Queenie had just said Singleton's and I had forgotten how many sections there were in the place. We bought our clothes for going to England there. It was one of those shops that sold everything, farm machinery, fuel, clothes, groceries. There was one counter for knitting wool and darning thread alone. Out at the back there was the bakery and beyond that the timber yard. And down at the end of a long lane with high walls on both sides there was a coal yard.

Whenever anyone came out the big double doors at the front I tried to look through to see if there was any sign of Hegarty. I didn't want to go in because Mr Singleton always stood in the centre of the shop greeting people and directing them to the goods they came to buy. He was a Protestant so he probably wouldn't have known me. Anyway I didn't want to walk in holding Hegarty's sandwiches. I decided to wait. I turned on the Diskette and looked about the place. There were no flags or bunting on Singleton's. All the other shops had at least one flag, and one shop – The Gem – had given over its entire window to a commemoration display. I walked over to have a look at it. There was a gilt-edged picture of Patrick Pearse in the centre, his face in side profile, and although the picture was in black and white, or more a brownish-grey, his cheeks were bright pink and his jacket was bright green. I could not decide if it was a drawing or a photograph. On both sides of the picture there were vases of artificial lilies, tall vases – much taller than the picture of Patrick Pearse. They were gold-coloured, a deep dark gold. And set into the middle of each was an oblong cameo with long-horned reddish-brown prairie cattle grazing by the marshy banks of a pale blue river. Up behind, pegged to a piece of string that ran from one side of the window to the other were six or seven magazines. I wondered why they had been left there. I idled through the titles trying to figure out if they were for sale or if they were in some way part of the display. *Moore's Almanac, Ireland's Own, The Messenger, The Far East.* I did not know what *Moore's Almanac* was and was trying to read the small print underneath the title when I heard Hegarty's voice from behind.

'That's a good kick up the arse for the Prods, isn't it?'

I looked at the display and agreed. And just in case he was in any doubt about my agreement, I laughed loudly and said that they deserved it. I think I would have said anything to avoid the way I had felt the day before.

Hegarty took out a packet of Craven A. He took two cigarettes out and handed one to me. Then he took a large square lighter from his pocket. It had the ace of diamonds on both sides, printed just like the card except much smaller. He held it at arm's length and flicked back the top in a swift movement, at the same time bringing his thumb down on the flint scraper. A long blue and green flame shot several inches into the air leaving a trail of black smoke as it steadied back down onto the wick. I had to turn my head sideways to light my cigarette and even then it got streaked with the black smoke. It was all deadpan, no looks, no checking, serious – a bit like one of those routines at the beginning of a judo bout.

'I heard the music from the yard. I said it was you, you should have come down. Come on. Bring that record player with you, here I'll get it.'

He walked across, picked up the Diskette, marched straight over to the shop and threw open the double doors. He stood there waiting for me to catch up.

'Here, turn it up, will you. It'll wake up a few people, they're all fucken dead in here.'

Keeping as far away from him as I could and wondering what else I could do to make it seem as if I wasn't with him, I told him that it was already up as much as it would go. Once inside he waited until everyone in the shop was looking and then stomped down the aisle. He passed Mr Singleton without looking and when he was a little bit beyond him and only barely out of his hearing he clearly said 'you big bollocks'. The Diskette swung by his side, throwing the music

forwards and backwards while his other arm swung extrava-
gantly as if he was marching. With a sudden fitful gesture he
drew that arm close to his side and, clenching his fist tightly,
brought it in, pressed it against his stomach and held it there.
Two fingers shot out mechanically, moving up and down
within a narrow space. Hegarty glanced back at Mr Singleton
and then across at me. I tried to smile but only managed a
thin smirk. I did not want to take part in whatever was going
on but I could see no way out.

Before we went to England, I had seen Mr Singleton as an
important man. I could not understand how he could be so
blatantly goaded. I did not want to join in, not because I had
any special regard for him, but because he was one of the
many fixed points on my landscape and I felt a wave of despair
as I saw those fixed points tumbling. One by one, our house,
Babs, Hegarty, they had all begun to shift.

As we approached the back door leading out to the coal
yard lane Hegarty handed me the Diskette. The woman in
charge of the nearby wool and thread counter kept her eyes
down as Hegarty held the door open, making sure she would
hear every last decibel of 'These Boots were Made for Walkin'.

All that afternoon I hung around the coal yard as he filled
up hundredweight sacks. The two brothers who had been
with him the day before came and went several times. The
older one drove the delivery van and the other one loaded up
the coal. They said 'fuck' to each other every so often but said
nothing to me. I watched with my back teeth clenched tightly
to form what I hoped was a world weary expression. I wanted
to appear slick and slightly hostile but no matter how well I
succeeded in my own mind, it made no difference. In their
eyes I was home from England and that was the beginning
and the end of it.

When Hegarty finished work we walked through the town
towards home. The carnival trucks had gone to the wrong
site and were reversing to a place where they could turn.

Everyone was out looking, giving their opinion and explaining what had happened. Hegarty stomped along with the Diskette, still at peak volume.

Dineen was there, clasping his hands, all businesslike and brisk as he made his way to the centre of the jam. The carnival troupe had been in the town several times before and were on their way to the place they had always used – unaware that a new site had been arranged. The carnival boss didn't seem to mind. He just nodded when Dineen had finished giving directions. They were all like that, casual and detached.

Dineen went to his car and came back to where we were standing with a few others. He had a card of paper badges, white lilies with the word *saoirse* written underneath. He pinned one onto the coat collar of a woman a few feet away from us and shook her hand. Someone laughed loudly at something he said. He had spoken without moving his lips, like a ventriloquist. That was the way he always spoke, giving the impression that there was someone watching him all the time waiting to catch him saying something he shouldn't be saying. Then he saw me and came rushing over with his hand stretched out.

The day before as we arrived at the train station, I had a very definite picture of what I was coming back to. I had thought so much about it. There were no uncertainties, no straggling questions, it was all in sharp focus, almost tangible. And even though things were turning out differently I must still have hoped that there would be a sudden change, a moment when the full impact of my return would dawn on everyone. I came closest to that when Dineen seized my hand and shook it with such force that I lost my balance.

'Where's Daddy? I hope he's all ready for Monday.'

His face was full of welcome.

'If it wasn't for this man's father and the likes of him,' he turned and looked at the people one by one, 'there would be no freedom to celebrate.'

I wanted to say a hundred things at once but only managed to say 'yes', leaving the rest to course rapidly around my head and blurt out in incoherent snatches as he pinned a lily onto my floral tie. He shook my hand again, held it and just looked straight at me.

'There mightn't be room for you all on the one run, we might have to do a second. I'll call about two, be sure and tell Daddy.'

He went over and pinned a lily badge on Hegarty's collar.

Just outside the town Hegarty stopped to light a cigarette. He handed me the Diskette and I stood holding it, thinking he was going to take it back – but he didn't. He stayed ahead the whole way back saying very little as if he did not want the conversation to pass a certain point.

10

I spent most of the following afternoon walking around with my father. With him I felt some of the excitement I had felt when Dineen shook hands with me. People greeted us, nodding and smiling, and two men stopped to talk to my father about the medal and the presentation ceremony. He smiled shyly and then began to explain that he was not involved in the 1916 rebellion – 'at least not in the Rising itself', he said, when he saw that they had taken him too literally.

'I was a sentry in 1922, on the lookout, over there.' He pointed towards the big tree. The night of the fire, December ...' But they were not interested in the facts. Their main interest was in guessing who the dignitary would be. One of them said that he had heard it was going to be a member of the government.

'Whoever it is,' the other man said, 'you can be sure he'll be high up, with the crowd that Dineen is in with these times.'

I waited while they talked on in a general way, and then drifted up to our house. My father followed a few minutes later and we stood there looking at it. There was nothing to say.

There was one old man sitting over at Moratorium Row. I decided to go over and take a look at the two bulky objects covered in black plastic. From the way I was examining them he must have decided that I did not know what they were.

'Statues. That one is Commandant Fran Dooley and the other is Mick Mackey. They're saying he was Dooley's lieutenant but I know for a fact that he wasn't.'

His voice was shaky and his eyes were raw and red like wounds.

'They won't be seen 'til Tuesday. There's too much going on there on Monday,' and he pointed across the moor towards the town. 'Too much going on with the medals, to draw a crowd out here. Too much. Too much to have anything here on Monday. We'll all be at the medals.' And he pointed to the town again.

I remembered Mick Mackey. He was the Mackeys' grandfather and he lived with them. They were in my class. They fought all the time. I could hardly believe that a statue had been made of him.

'Three hundred pound each, made above in Dublin by a statue maker.'

I was still examining them when my father came over. He obviously knew all about them because he paid no heed to them. He and the old man did not speak. It was as if everything they might have said to each other had already been said.

That evening Hegarty called for me to go to the carnival. It took us well over an hour to get there. It was two miles beyond the town which itself was almost three miles away. A thin drizzle, almost indistinguishable from fog, clung with the lightness of a spider's web to my clothes and made Hegarty's face red and sort of luminous.

Once we were at the far side of the town we began to hear snatches of the carnival music in the distance. Whenever the sound disappeared we filled in the gaps, singing and acting as if we were playing the instruments. Hegarty did the brass and I did the lead guitar. As we got nearer the music grew louder and clearer and there were less and less opportunities to fill in the missing bits. So we just sang along, stopping every so often to act out the intense parts; parts like that pause in 'Only the Lonely' when it sounds as if Roy Orbison is so overcome with pain that he may not be able to bridge the gap between the final 'Only' and the final 'The Lonely'. Then he just about makes it and on we go in the drizzle, Hegarty, Roy Orbison and me – pressing my fingers into the frets of an imaginary guitar.

Hegarty knew the words much better than I did. This came as a surprise because all the time I knew him he had hardly any interest in music at all. I was reluctant – more than reluctant, I refused – to believe that he had become interested since I left.

But during those years Hegarty had gone to every dance for miles around and so he knew all the songs, not just the hits of the time because the bands, showbands, played everything from Viennese waltzes to Rhythm and Blues, Rock 'n' Roll, Swing numbers from the war era, Dixieland, and lots of Country and Western. The carnival music, broadcast from a single loud speaker tied with binding twine to the top of a pole, spanned the same era.

I listened to Hegarty sing along with Helen Shapiro. 'Walkin' Back to Happiness'. He included every oh-yeah and every oop-ah with such precise timing that I stopped trying to keep up. Next came 'That'll be the day', followed by 'It's Now or Never'. All the time I kept hoping that the next one would be one I knew well, and I knew almost everything that had been released from about Christmas 1963 to that very moment. They played nothing from those years. I was saying this to Hegarty as we walked into the carnival field when he cut in sharply.

'That's not my fucken fault, what are you telling me for? Why don't you tell them? Look.'

He pointed to the loud speaker and to the single black cable leading to a caravan. It was up the field a bit, set apart from the rest of the carnival. There was a hatch in the side facing us, with a glass screen – like a chip van. With all the razzmatazz on the way in I had not noticed that at the top of the field, set among huge spreading trees, was a house so full of light that when I first saw it I thought it was on fire. Somewhere at the back of my mind I had a vague memory of it and still I had the sensation of seeing it for the first time.

The girl behind the glass screen in the caravan had her shoulders hunched up, holding her cardigan in place. It might easily have slipped down her back – it was so soft. And the colours, candy floss, peppermint, lime and pale violet merged into each other. Her hair was short and brushed down into a flat fringe that did not end where fringes usually do. It curved down the side of her face, almost touching the outer tips of her eyebrows and then turned in, finishing in sharp points near the sides of her mouth. She was browsing through a magazine and every time she turned a page her head turned with it, moving in a slow luxurious way, as though she was sinking back into a sea of pillows.

We stood looking at her through the glass screen, thinking that at any moment she would look up. When, after a minute or so we were still standing there looking and she was still turning the pages in slow motion, Hegarty tapped the glass. She lifted her head but kept her eyes on the magazine for as long as possible. Then, still not looking up at us, she stretched her hand out to the hatch clasp and left it there until the record, spinning on the turntable beside her, ended. When the hatch opened the air filled with a warm scent, an even blend of aniseed and new fabric.

Although we had been waiting there for several minutes, neither of us spoke. Then without the slightest warning Hegarty turned to me – his expression full of accusation.

'Go on, say what you said to me about the records.'

She looked at me and then out over me and down towards the rest of the carnival.

'It was nothing. I was only wondering if you, if there was anything from the charts?'

She reached for a brown cardboard box on a ledge behind her and without speaking handed it to me, closed the hatch and started putting on another record, all in one continuous movement. The box was full of singles, thrown together with crumpled record covers. I picked one up, all ready to say I liked it, all ready to bring it to an end. But I had never heard of it and had only vaguely heard of the singer, Irving Berlin. I looked into the box thinking desperate thoughts. Maybe the caravan would fill with flames, no, just smoke, and I would suddenly have to fling the box of records into the night, wrench the hatch from its fittings and save her. Hegarty's thoughts were not so hopelessly disguised.

'Would you get up on her? She's asking for it, did you see the way she handed you the records?'

The hatch slid across. I grabbed a record and tried to read the title but the label was so worn that it was impossible.

'Here's your chance,' Hegarty muttered under his breath.

I handed her the record and the box and without looking or speaking she took it and lined it up to drop onto the turntable. She stretched her hand out slowly and began closing the hatch with the same bored movements. In a single stroke, Hegarty's hand appeared, pressed flat against the glass, a movement so swift that it seemed violent by contrast.

'He's from England,' Hegarty roared, determined to have his say before the hatch closed. He was pointing at me, with his finger held like a gun, almost touching the top of my ear. The hatch closed.

'And now a request, his very own choice, from someone who is,' she drew her head back a little from the microphone, 'here on holiday from England.'

She replaced the microphone beside the record player and continued reading the magazine.

Her voice rang out above the carnival noise. It sounded more like an announcement than a request. The crackling sounds that followed settled somewhere below the screeching of the bumper cars. I began to think about being back in London. When the music started I was beyond caring that it was probably the worst record in the box. No other record in the world could have made my choice seem more out of date. It was from the musical *Oklahoma*: 'When I take her out in my surrey with the fringe on top'.

'Did you hear that? You heard that didn't you, she's playing it for you, you'd be a right fool not to take a hint.'

'I can't. I promised ...' and before I said the words 'my girlfriend', I hesitated, aware of the effect they would have on Hegarty. As soon as I had said them I wanted to take them back. I repeated to myself what I had said, searching the words for a loophole, a flaw that I could exploit to change the meaning and so twist the lie into something that had been awkwardly put and, as a result, misunderstood by Hegarty. There were no loopholes. 'My girlfriend.' It was as clear as it could be, but I was temporarily saved from witnessing the full impact it had by the arrival of the commemoration committee for the official opening of the carnival.

They had come down the avenue from the house with the blazing windows, which, after I asked twice, Hegarty grudgingly told me belonged to the Dineens. I wanted to ask him more about it, but he had become sullen and so I held back, figuring out for myself when the Dineens had moved out of the town. I had not noticed that the entrance gate to the carnival field was also the entrance gate to the big house. As I followed the line of the avenue from that gate to the dark

trees on the hill, I wondered if there was any way out of the
fix I found myself in. I wished above all else that I had not
used the word girlfriend. No matter how much I tossed it
about in my head, dividing it up into girl and friend, it
continued to have the same meaning. It conjured up a whole
way of life, which there and then in the middle of that field,
seemed unquestionably foreign. I kept imagining two people,
each with a stripey straw drinking out of the same glass,
confidently staring at each other. Dates, telephones, dancing,
all so easy. I had given Hegarty the impression that I had that
kind of life. And because I was home from England he was
all too ready to believe me.

As we watched the commemoration committee get out of
their cars I considered telling Hegarty the whole story of Noe,
Lil and Gus's daughter from upstairs. She was the girl I
had in mind, not when I first used the word girlfriend but
immediately afterwards when I wanted to play down what I
had said. She was two years older than me and had a boy-
friend, which made her 'a girlfriend'. She went to the same
school as me and left the house more or less at the same time
every morning. The big question on my mind, whenever I met
her at the bus stop, was how near one person could stand to
another without rousing their suspicions. Every day I went
through the same routine, edging myself towards Noe in
centimetres, imagining that because she did not move away
she was interested. I didn't know what to do. I was definitely
not capable of pouncing. I looked at Hegarty, full sure that
he was a pouncer and full sure that he would not know what
I was on about if I told him about the bus stop. He was
pretending to be all interested in the arrival of the commemoration committee but it was easy to see that he had
become distant. I kept on trying to think of ways of changing
the Noe story to fit the ending I had given it – me promising
to be loyal. But the more I thought about it the more impossible that became. I even considered telling the whole truth

and then, when I had given up searching for a way out I suddenly came up with the idea of saying that the promise I had made was to myself. I had promised myself to be loyal to my girlfriend. Brilliant. And it was not a big step from there to a point where it would become obvious to Hegarty that she wasn't yet my girlfriend.

I went through the whole thing real fast. It was all fine until I got to the most recent part, the Saturday before we left, the day we went to Balham, when I got the Beatle suit and the Beatle boots.

The caravan in the front garden was parked so near the window facing my bed that it blocked all the light coming into the room. It made no difference whether the curtains were open or closed. And so they stayed closed all the time except for the two weeks in the summer when Gus and Lil took the caravan off on holiday.

During the winter Noe went into it a lot, sometimes with her friends, sometimes on her own. She would bounce into the lounge, turn on the record player, close her eyes, softly grip one side of her lower lip with her front teeth and dance, swaying slowly from side to side. The whole of the previous winter I had watched through a tiny chink in the curtains, watched and watched and watched. I knew every pin-up on the lounge wall and had bigger versions of the same groups, The Beatles, Gerry and the Pacemakers, Freddie and the Dreamers, pinned to the back of the wardrobe against which my own bed stood.

The evening we got back from Balham, I went to try on my Beatle suit and had just put it on when the caravan lit up. In a moment of abandonment I opened the curtains, a single swooping move, keeping my eyes closed and dancing to the record Noe had put on. I didn't open my eyes and hoped as I raised my hands above my head that she would see all the pin-ups behind me, all her favourites, with me among them in my Beatle suit, almost as if I was one of them. I kept my eyes closed for a long time, as though that was part of the dance.

When I opened them, as the record came to an end, she was gone. A few days later I was on the boat home.

I had heard little of the speeches but the cheer from the small crowd gathered around was so loud when Dineen finished that I knew something out of the ordinary had been said. I did not want to ask Hegarty what it was and so I tried to make sense of the bits I had caught, filling in the gaps by listening to the people around me. But I didn't get much because a whole bunch of them, nearly all, ran down to the bumpers, shouting and roaring and pushing.

Hegarty watched until they reached the bumpers. When he spoke he gazed around in a general sort of way as if he was not speaking to anyone in particular.

'Not much point going down there, with that crowd. The hour'll be up before they've all had goes.'

I followed him down to the rifle range, rehearsing the Noe story, anxiously waiting for an opportunity to tell it. I gathered from what the range keeper said that the commemoration committee promised to pay for everything at the carnival for the first hour. Hegarty loaded the gun like a real hot shot. The range keeper was very small, he had no neck and his arms were so short that I could not imagine him clapping his hands or holding a ball. He had to get up on an empty beer crate to put the target cards in place. Hegarty took his first shot as soon as the small man got down from the crate. I thought he would say something to Hegarty, tell him to be careful or give him some sort of warning. But he just slipped to the side, smiling.

Two shots followed in quick succession and then Hegarty's voice full of triumph.

'Bull's eye – third shot lucky.'

He handed me the gun while the small man took down the target card. As he waddled towards us Hegarty pointed to the prizes, telling him that he wanted the set of red-handled screwdrivers.

The small man put the target card on the counter, smiling even as he told Hegarty that the shot was partly on the edge of the circle and could not be counted as a bull's eye. Very willingly I took Hegarty's side, pointing and nodding as the target card went back and forth between them. But the small man, still smiling, remained unmoved. He put three pellets on the counter and told Hegarty to try his luck again.

'Give me that fucken gun,' Hegarty snarled as he snatched it from me, making it clear, as he wedged the rifle stock into his shoulder, that he was aiming at the prizes. There was no time to consider any of the stray impulses I felt; impulses like pulling the gun out of his hand, telling him about Noe or saying I was going. I was more relieved than anything else, when the small plate at the top of the prize board shattered. It had happened and there was nothing I could do about it. One piece was left dangling on the prize board. I had noticed the plate when Hegarty was pointing at the screwdrivers. It had gold writing on it, 'A mother's love is a blessing', and tangled in among the letters were flowers and rushes. The small man was still smiling. I think he must have been afraid because he said nothing and did not move from his position at the side of the counter. Hegarty surveyed the prizes and as he did I wondered if he was going to pick another one off. There were lots of them, pink teddies, a clock set into an owl's body, big scissors, John F. and Jacqueline Kennedy in a twin cameo frame. He put the gun down and took out a packet of cigarettes, lit one slowly and walked away.

I stood watching him jostle his way to the front of the crowd at the bumper cars, where, from his gestures and laughter I could tell he was describing what had happened at the rifle range. Some of them looked over but he didn't, he just went on taking shots with an imaginary gun. I dawdled around for a bit, thinking of the distance stretching between me and them. I wanted to stop thinking about that distance and walk over and join in the scramble for the bumper cars but I couldn't. I knew now it was impossible to step in and just take up where I had left off. Once formed, it seemed as if that thought had been there all along. It was so familiar that I could trace it all the way back along a thin broken line through the two and a half years in England, back to the time before we left when I first glimpsed the possibility of losing the world around me. Now suddenly it was certain, a fixed point around which all other thoughts seemed to revolve. And spinning outwards, way out of reach, were all the hopes and half-hopes which had shored up the belief that nothing had been lost.

I drifted down towards the gate, seeing for the first time that it was a big formal entrance. The granite pillars, like monuments, had large metal birds on top. The silvery flecks in the granite glistened as the carnival lights swung back and forth in the wind. I traced the course of the avenue back up the hill to the dark trees and the house with the windows full of soft yellow light. I gazed at that light, still wondering why it was familiar, trying all the time to remember the house as it was before we went to England. But there were endless blurred thoughts mingling with the clamour of the carnival.

From the distance the streetlamps of the town formed a long line of hard white light, a line that broke into single pools of light as I got nearer. The music got less and less distinct until all that remained was a low thudding sound which kept getting swept away by sudden bursts of wind. I looked back at the big house several times, searching for the memory that made it so familiar. Only when it was well out of sight and I was walking through the town did I first begin to sense that I would not find the memory I was seeking by searching my own past. Still, it had all the features of a memory, the great scene from my father's past, an event I had known about for such a long time that I imagined I had

114

actually witnessed it and so it had come to reside in my memory.

High up above and all around me the commemoration flags and bunting were flapping wildly in the April winds, celebrating freedom and independence. It was a place where burning houses had marked the dawning of a new era, but one which, there and then, seemed full of hollow claims. My future was in England and what I wanted to do most, as things became increasingly clear, was to go back – return to London and just get on with things, unburdened by those hollow claims that kept my father looking back.

11

Dineen arrived at precisely half past two. The dignitary sitting in the passenger seat was not how I had imagined him. He had glasses, round-rimmed black and mustard glasses. His face was shiny smooth and he smiled, all friendly, listening in a very concentrated way to the arrangements Dineen was making with Bríd about bringing her, my father and me first – and then coming back for Queenie and my sisters. When the arrangements were sorted out we got into the car. The dignitary turned around and held out his hand which Bríd and my father both went to shake at the same time. We all laughed, breathing in the fumes of the lavender odour blocks which had been placed all over the car for the occasion. The dignitary spoke about the commemoration ceremonies and said that they were a credit to the committee. We all agreed. He asked me about school, what class was I in, did I know the date of the Battle of Hastings? Dineen kept on saying 'yep', even when there was nothing to agree to. He must have glanced at us in the rear view mirror a hundred times in the first few minutes of that journey. At one stage, while he was telling us about the dignitary, he looked in the mirror for the best part of a minute, letting the car drift to the other side of the road. He told us that the dignitary was a high-ranking member of the Land Commission with particular responsibility for our area.

'There'll hardly be a person here today who wasn't delighted to see his signature at some stage in their lives and I'll tell you, there'll be a few hoping to see that signature yet – on divide claims they have made.'

The dignitary said nothing. He didn't even smile when Dineen looked across at him, naming people he knew were looking for Land Commission divides. When we got out of the car my father was escorted off by two men with green arm bands and lily badges. One of them came back and started urging people to sit. Bríd was led to the front row and I followed. As we sat down my father walked onto the platform guided by the official. Some people began clapping but the official, with his arms stretched out and his hands moving up and down, got them to stop. Then he picked up the microphone tapped it and said 'save the clapping till later'. Everybody clapped. A man, somewhere towards the back, roared, 'Give us a song, Dooley.' The official pretended that he was going to sing and then left. My father smiled and looked down at us.

Four or five nuns were led to our row and directed to the empty seats on the inside. Each of them whispered 'excuse me' as she passed and when they were all sitting down they took turns to lean over and shake hands with Bríd and then me. Bríd explained to them that the seats to my right were reserved for her sister and her daughters. While she spoke she tugged the hem of her skirt, trying to get it to stretch down to her knees, but every time she moved it slipped back up. Eventually she picked up her handbag from the ground and placed it on the gap between the hem of her skirt and her knees. She smiled at me and tilting her head very slightly in the direction of the nuns drew me into a conspiracy with an expression of false modesty.

I heard Queenie's voice from behind and turned around just in time to see her walk solemnly down towards us carrying my sister's dancing costumes, nodding to all the people seated on either side. As she moved forwards her pace slowed down and her nod became a bow, directed alternately and in slow motion, to the people on her right and then to those on her left. Gretta walked behind mimicking her movements and giggling. Agnes stayed well back, looking up at my father. Queenie beckoned to her to hurry and then ushered them both into the seats beside us, while she made elaborate signs to Bríd about how Gretta and Agnes ought to sit so that the dancing costumes would not touch the ground. The nuns leaned over to shake hands with Queenie. As they stretched across they whispered compliments about my father, about me, about my sisters, each following so fast on the next that these compliments formed a single drawn out hissing sound which shot from one end of our row to the other.

People behind started clapping as the relations of some of the other men arrived. My father was still the only one on the stage and he kept glancing to the side waiting for the others to be led out. When the first of them walked on, escorted across the stage by a man with a green arm band whom I hadn't seen before, my father smiled broadly and stood up to shake hands. Soon more of them arrived, old men shakily making their way across the stage and then standing to attention like soldiers waiting to be inspected. My father offered his chair to a man with two walking sticks who got so angry that for a second or two I thought he was going to use them to hit my father.

I knew my father would not sit down again. He didn't seem at all bothered by what had happened. But he must have thought I was because he smiled down at me and winked, full of the day and all that was going on. There, in among the old men, he looked young and alert. I was not used to thinking of him as young and smiled up at him, pleased to think that even though he was almost sixty he was not an old man.

When Dineen led the dignitary onto the stage everyone clapped loudly and just as that clapping began to die down the Canon walked onto the stage led by two men with arm-bands. The clapping took off again and continued as the Canon gestured to someone at the side of the stage who, from the way the Canon was beckoning, was unwilling to come out. After a minute another priest walked onto the stage. He was wearing a full length skirted coat and a cape which went down as far as his elbows. He had a weary freckled face and a pair of gold rimmed glasses pressed very close to his eyes. The clapping surged for a moment and then trailed off. The Canon later announced that this priest, Monsignor Mullen, was on holiday from Kenya where he had been working on the missions for thirty-nine years.

With very little warning the Canon blessed himself and looked out over the people. Everyone quickly tried to kneel down except the nuns who sat on the very edges of their chairs, each with her hands joined evenly and firmly together. When the prayer started they brought their hands right up to the tips of their noses and with their eyes shut let their lips move as though they were nibbling the tops of their index fingers. Queenie, who had grabbed the dancing costumes from Gretta and Agnes as they knelt down, was trying to join her hands without bunching the costumes up. Some of the old men towards the front of the stage were kneeling on one knee, resting both their hands and what looked like their full weight on that same knee. Monsignor Mullen looked around at everything and everyone. His head was shaking slightly, but very fast. I wouldn't have noticed that except for the quivering glint of light on the rim of his glasses.

Dineen began his speech by saying that it was a great day for Ireland. 'Great,' he said again in a loud voice. 'Great to be able to look back on fifty years of freedom – fifty years since the glorious blow for independence was struck against an empire that had kept us in slavery for over seven hundred years.'

Some people began to clap but before their clapping got properly underway Dineen started to speak again.

'And it's a great day for us too, a great day because the people we have to thank for that freedom, at least some of them, are standing here behind me.'

He tried to speak above the applause, but had to give in. Then he stood back reluctantly and, turning towards the men behind him, flung his arm in their direction. Everyone clapped vigorously and Dineen bowed his head.

All together the old men drew breath and stood to attention. Their gaze travelled out above us to some fixed point in the distance. And they stayed like that, without moving. It was as if they had become a photograph of themselves.

Dineen, with his arm still held out in their direction, told everyone that generations of Irishmen and women would remember their bravery. I thought that some of them would look down. I was certain that my father would and I kept waiting for that moment – but he, like all the others, had gone into a trance.

Dineen's head swung to the right and with a very stern expression he beckoned someone at the side of the stage. A girl, his daughter, Bríd whispered, walked on carrying a tray of medals.

'Everybody sitting in front of me,' Dineen announced, 'knows the name of this man here on my left and if they don't know his name, then they shouldn't be here today, so they shouldn't.'

We all laughed and the dignitary smiled as he moved a little to the side making room for Dineen's daughter.

When they were all set, standing in the way Dineen wanted them to stand, he leaned across and in a very official way shook hands with the dignitary, welcoming him on behalf of the commemoration committee. Then without letting the dignitary's hand go, he began to speak, slowly pronouncing the words and charging them with such conviction that each one sounded like a statement in itself.

'The hand I am holding here,' and he squeezed the dignitary's hand firmly 'is a hand I'm proud to shake, a hand that many people here today . . .' and he stopped, giving way to the clapping and the shouting.

Every time he went to speak the clapping and the shouting got louder and not until it was clear that he wanted to move on to the presentation of the medals did it begin to ebb.

'Now, Ladies and Gentlemen, on behalf of the commemoration committee, we will honour each of these brave men with the Medal of Freedom. It is a very beautiful medal.' Saying the word 'beautiful' again and pronouncing it with a 'd' in the middle, 'Beaudiful,' he held it up for us to see. Then letting it dangle for a moment or two in front of us he described what was depicted on it.

'On this side there is Cúchulain, the greatest of all Irish warriors, someone many of these men behind me here could stand beside with pride. And here on the other side we have our President, His Excellency, Mr Éamon de Valera, who has done more than any living man to free us from England.'

Each freedom medal hung from a green, white and gold ribbon which Dineen, followed by his daughter, handed to the dignitary. Standing in front of the first man, the dignitary held the medal for a moment then slowly and carefully raised it up over the old man's head and ceremoniously brought it down to rest on his chest. The man did not look down. He just stared into the middle distance and that's what every one of them did, they just stared. It was as if the freedom medal had the power to paralyse anyone around whose neck it was hung. I drifted away with that thought for a moment or two, imagining them all unable to hear, or to see, or to speak or to move.

My father was last to get a medal. By the time his turn came I had given up hoping he would act in any way different to the others.

Dineen walked solemnly back to the microphone. Before he spoke he nodded to his daughter, indicating that she should leave. With a series of fast eye movements she tried to tell him that there were some medals left on the tray. Covering the microphone with his hand and speaking in a muted, urgent whisper, he said, 'would you for God's sake go.'

A sudden burst of dazzling sunshine filled the sky with strands of luminous pale light which shone directly into the eyes of the men on stage, bouncing off their medals, glistening and shooting back out in silvery white lines of light. Some of the men blinked and others, determined to hold their gaze, squinched up their eyes until they went watery. I felt certain that they would not be able to hold out much longer, certain that they could not remain like that, forever frozen in time. But they went on standing, spell-bound by loyalty to a past they shared.

Eventually, when Dineen mentioned one or two of them by name, some of the others began to lose their glazed look. As he spoke about the events we were commemorating it became clear that he was not as concerned with the 1916 rebellion as he was with the events that took place afterwards. Several of them began to nod as they listened to him talk about 1922, the year of the great fire. At that point my father turned to look at a man whose name was mentioned, visibly pleased that so much was being said about an event in which he himself had taken part. All along he had been worried about getting a medal for the 1916 rebellion. He had gone to great lengths to point out to people during the previous few days that he was too young to know what was going on then, but that he had been on the lookout, a sentry, on the night of the great fire six years later.

Dineen said nothing about the part he had played himself and afterwards when people were standing around talking they said that it was modesty that held him back. But it was clear from the way they said it that they were a bit disappointed. What he had done made the best known of all the stories from those times. He was the one who had started the fire. More than once I had heard him tell the story of Mrs Forestock in flames, running around the room grabbing up the photographs of her husband and her son. When Dineen had his dance band he used to do a stand-up comic piece and what the crowd always called for was Mrs Forestock on fire.

The ceremony ended with a blessing from the Canon who said he felt sure that God had guided the Irish people along the road to freedom and that we had Him to thank more than anyone else. Some people clapped and some people blessed themselves.

When my father came down from the stage he told us that he and the other men, with their families, had been invited to the Canon's house to have a cup of tea. Queenie's face lit up but suddenly tensed with alarm when Bríd, who was examining my father's medal, said that it would be an ideal place for Gretta and Agnes to change into their dancing costumes. Queenie made every effort to hide the fear with which that suggestion filled her, but her eyes had become fixed like the eyes of a stuffed bird and no matter how hard she tried she did not seem able to regain normal eye movements. She smiled, but that only made her fear more apparent because her smiling mouth and startled eyes made her look like a puppet whose facial movements had gone askew. Anyway it didn't matter what she did because by that stage we all knew that she had lost her battle to keep her views in check.

'I mean you can't do that, you can't, let the girls change in the Canon's house. I mean where would they change? In what room?'

Nobody answered and it might have ended there if she hadn't gone on to point out how improper it was even to think of asking the Canon to let two young girls change in his house. Bríd went to say something but Queenie cut in full of indignation, in a voice that was shrill and wobbly.

'If those girls' behaviour in my house since they came is anything to go by then we need say no more.'

My father walked away and I followed.

The Canon's house was spotlessly clean but the smell was not one of cleanliness. It was a metallic smell, a bit like the smell from the inside of an empty biscuit tin. In the big room to the right there were four women standing behind a table full of crockery and iced cakes. Each of them held a large stainless steel tea pot, waiting for the go-ahead from the Canon's housekeeper. She stood in the middle of the room with a tray full of triangular sandwiches. She smiled at my father as he approached and keeping her lips together as if she was sucking a straw, said 'congratulations'. I was glad to be with him. I had never been in the Canon's house and neither had he. He confided this to a woman who came over to us with a blue rimmed cup and saucer in one hand and a sugar bowl in the other.

'Very few had until recently,' she whispered, adding that the rules about who could and who couldn't be let into the Canon's house had only been changed very recently by Vatican Two. The fawn-coloured tea lapped from side to side, each time leaving a thin oily film clinging just below the blue rim.

As she talked about the commemoration ceremonies a rainbow of colour filled the doorway and Agnes and Gretta tumbled into the room in full dancing costume. They skipped over towards us followed by Monsignor Mullen who was smiling and nodding while Bríd told him about the South East London Set Dancing Competition in which Gretta had come second the previous December. He said he would like a photograph of us to take back to Mombasa. We all went outside and stood on the steps. Months later, when we had forgotten all about that photograph, it arrived from Mombasa in a frame of intricately carved ivory. With it were other photographs of the commemoration ceremony and a photograph of some children in Monsignor Mullen's mission school – dancing. We learned from his letter that they were doing The Walls of Limerick. Bríd put the framed photograph up on the mantelpiece in the flat. When I saw it for the first time that afternoon all that it portrayed seemed to have settled into a much more distant past.

I did not ask where Queenie was. I sensed from the confidential way Bríd spoke to my father and from the bits of that conversation I overhead on the way over to the dance marquee that she was talking about Queenie. But she wasn't taking her side in the way she had since we arrived. I also sensed, from the very pointed way we seemed to be regrouping under Bríd's direction, that she had run out of whatever it took to stay on good terms with Queenie. That was one of those things which once sensed, immediately becomes an absolute fact, illuminating a host of other facts. And there, holding them all together, was the knowledge that I was looking forward to going back.

12

The entrance to the marquee was through a small opening in the canvas where a flap was pulled to the side and tied back with a frayed rope. Directly in front was another flap which I had to push aside to get in. Inside – and still stooping with the inner flap resting on my back – I raised my head and stopped to take in the enormous space. Gretta ducked down and edged her way through on my right while Agnes pushed from behind telling me to move on. They both ran straight past the two men sitting at the felt-covered card table, who smiled and nodded the second my father went to tell them that the girls were included in the family ticket he bought.

Several card tables had been pushed together and covered with lining paper to form a long counter. It ran from the left of the stage down to another canvas flap with a hand-written sign, saying 'Ladies', pinned above it. Although there might have been twenty or thirty people gathered in front of the counter the marquee still seemed empty. A tall man with an oily quiff slid through a flap behind the counter, carrying a crate of bottles. He was followed by an older man, also carrying a crate but with a lot less ease. For the next half-hour or so they came in and out through the flap, bringing crate after crate until they had built a high wall behind the counter. They then started lifting cardboard boxes of glasses from under the counter and in a series of slick movements took the glasses out four at a time. There was a swerving rhythm to those movements which kept us all watching.

Running along the opposite side of the marquee was a long row of empty benches. Bríd sat down while Gretta and Agnes practised their steps and poses in front of her. They spun around each other, effortlessly arriving at a formal back to back pose from which they then sprang forward into a different series of loops that brought them further and further apart. And just when it seemed that neither of them could possibly know what the other was doing they arrived back at the precise position from which they had started.

The bar was officially opened by Dineen about an hour and a half after we arrived. There were two drinks; ale and lemonade, with one hundred and forty-four cases of each all paid for by the committee. Lots of people around the marquee were trying to work out how many bottles of ale there were per person. The answers differed but all of them were above ten.

With two opened bottles of ale in each hand and an index finger between each bottle, the barmen managed to fill eight glasses at a time which worked out at about sixteen glasses a minute. Someone near us said that if they kept pouring at that pace then there was enough free ale to last for over two and a half hours. At first they were not able to keep up and every few minutes or so glasses fighting for a refill smashed as they collided under a pouring bottle. When this happened, the barmen just went on opening bottles, one, two, three, four and with a quick twist of the wrist poured without looking up, confident that new glasses would arrive to be filled. The bar counter was so ale soaked that the green dye from the card tables beneath ran into the cream lining paper. The globes of sweat under the barmen's arms spread to their waists and the younger one had to flick back his oily quiff more and more frequently. After a while they began to look up as they poured, not because the pace changed but because they got careless. They calmly surveyed the crowds milling in front of them and didn't move a single face muscle when the band entered. Led by the drummer, who threw a cymbal high into the air, letting it crash to the floor, Roy and the Red Aces moved quickly to the stage. They were wearing wide-lapelled crimson tuxedos braided with purple satin, with bow ties of the same material. Two small boys carried a crate of ale over to the stage and in between hurried swigs, The Aces, as everyone called them, pushed jack plugs into amps, tapped mikes, winked at groups of girls mooning about below them and ran their fingers up and down their guitar frets.

Roy glanced from side to side and then, tapping his black patent shoes, he brought the band into a countdown routine. Three ... Two ... One for the money, Two for the show – and the crowd pounced into action, jiving in a way I had only seen people jive in Elvis films. As I watched I imagined that my Beatle suit and boots marked me out as a prophet of fashion. But fairly soon I began to see that nothing was in fashion or out of fashion and what people probably saw when they looked at me was not my Beatle suit or my Beatle boots but just someone home from England.

They had not been playing for very long when Roy announced that couples taking part in the twisting competition should line up on both sides of the stage. A big space was cleared and the first ten couples, bobbing up and down in anticipation, were ushered in. I stood up and went over, edging my way through the crowd until I got to a place where I could see what was going on.

'Ready,' Roy shouted, extending the 'dy' until it merged into 'Come on let's twist again like we did . . . '

The competing couples twisted in every direction. They were twisting on their heels and on their toes, tilting forwards and then backwards to a point from which some of them could not work their way up without putting one hand on the ground. I followed every move they made, hoping above all else to mask the growing panic I felt as it dawned on me that there had been some sort of mix-up about the competition. Dreading what I might see when I turned to look at them, I stole a quick sideways glance at my sisters. But they were just sitting on the bench between Bríd and my father, swinging their legs to the music. Bríd sat smiling and my father sat motionless while his freedom medal shone like a distant light-house under the swaying electric light.

I wanted to save them. I wanted to rush them out before they knew what was happening. But I saw Bríd whisper something to my father who then looked over at the door. I was very relieved when they got up to leave. But just then the music stopped and, like people stranded in a game of musical chairs, they stood there while Roy, prompted by one of the Aces, spoke to them from the stage. Holding the mike high in the air he asked the competitors to make way. Slowly the dancers parted, forming a corridor to a clearing in the middle of the floor. Agnes clung to Bríd like a barnacle but Gretta cast her eyes downwards and then coyly looked up, pretending to be bored by what was going on. Several times the band started a basic reel routine, a few guitar plucks, a little tapping on the drums and a fading base – giving way to a second request from Roy.

'All dressed up and nowhere to go, make way, Ladies and Gentlemen, make way for the high stepping colleens.'

The music started again and as the tempo quickened my father moved nearer to Bríd. Suddenly they both reached together to catch Gretta as she took her first step forward.

Aware of their efforts to stop her, she zoomed up through the clearing in the crowd and shot straight into the middle of the dance floor. Her first few steps were formal, keeping pace with the music, but it soon became obvious that the band could only play the opening bars of the reel because they played those bars over and over again before they slipped into another piece. And it turned out that the little bit of the reel they had played was the beginning of a medley of about ten short pieces, each one sliding directly into the next.

Straight away I recognized the second, 'You ain't nothin' but a hound-dog'. Other pieces like the cancan chorus were familiar in a vague way. Gretta did not change her basic reel stop for Hound-dog, but instead leapt high into the air, shooting up like a sudden blaze, and landed spinning into a dizzy furl in which all the reds, yellows, blues and greens of her costume whisked into a single blur of flaming colour. When the band broke into the cancan she stood still for a second, quickly checked the space in front of her and charged forward gathering all the momentum she could. Three full cart wheels followed. With each one her dress fanned out and fell and the marquee resounded with hoots and yelps. The medley ended with 'Rock around the Clock', to which Gretta did a series of splays and splits, finally ending with some kind of Spanish castanet dance that involved flicking her head from side to side, stamping her feet and clicking her fingers. When she bowed at the end, she backed away touching the floor with hand flourishes. The crowd cheered and cheered until the cheering became a sort of game between them and Gretta – who went on bowing. Everywhere, all around me, the people turned to each other and nodded, home from England.

In a welter of applause and shouts, she backed over towards my father, Bríd and Agnes.

A little later, as part of a carefully controlled broad sweeping survey of the marquee, I saw them leaving. Agnes walked ahead and Bríd and my father followed with Gretta in between them, each holding one of her arms as if she were a convict being led out of court. I resisted the urge to go on looking at them and just continued my survey of the marquee. Pre-occupied by thoughts about what was happening to Gretta I did not at first recognize Hegarty, at the other side of the marquee, making signs, nodding and throwing his head to one side, indicating that he wanted me to go outside. He must have thought I did not understand because his signs grew more pronounced. Then he began to mouth words, twisting his chin and slowly parting his lips until his whole face became an open mouth. I smiled and then started to laugh as he held an imaginary bottle up, tilted it towards his open mouth and went through the motions of pouring. He even stopped to make glugging movements with his throat. His next gesture was an unmistakable invitation to go outside.

Trying not to trip over the tent ropes I followed Hegarty. We went down the side and around the back, directly behind the stage, to where the light cast by the marquee divided into two distinct blocks on either side of a small shed. We picked out steps over chunks of broken wall and mortar around to the far side of the shed. It was impossible to see if there was a door or not, there was just a pool of darkness bounded on either side by the blocks of light. Back behind, Roy and the Aces were playing 'From a Jack to a King' and the sound bounced off the wall of the shed in such clear tones that I felt as if I was standing on the stage in the middle of it.

I thought I heard Hegarty say something but I wasn't sure so I moved up closer to him, expecting that if he had he would repeat it. Instead, I heard a clinking noise coming from the ground in front of me and looking into the darkness saw two figures leaning against the shed wall. When a hand offering me an opened bottle made its way forward through the darkness I began to understand what was going on. The ale tasted sour and under different circumstances I might not have felt obliged to take a second swig. Within minutes the hand came out of the darkness again. Another bottle. I did not like the taste but was able to swallow it by putting the neck of the bottle on the back of my tongue and just pouring. After a while I lost whatever sense of taste I had and then stopped thinking about it altogether. I wanted to say something, nothing in particular, I just wanted to hear my voice, to make sure it was me thinking those thoughts. But I didn't want to be the first to speak. Another bottle came from the darkness and I heard my voice saying thanks. The word seemed to come from the stage, amplified and full of implications which I did not intend it to have.

'How many fucken bottles have you drunk?'

'Three,' I answered before I realized that Hegarty's question was directed at the others.

'There's twenty-nine left,' one of them said.

'And there'll soon be twenty fucken eight,' the other added as he flung an empty bottle into the light cast by the marquee.

'You're right fucken bollockses,' Hegarty snarled in a tone I knew was friendly, even though it sounded like an accusation.

I do not know how long we stayed there. Long enough for me to learn that the two figures were the same two brothers I had seen on the green the afternoon we arrived. They had helped the barmen with the crates of ale and had been slipped a case. One of them said that he was thinking of going to England and in a roundabout way started asking me questions. Each time I went to answer I started laughing. It was as if I was about to tell a joke and couldn't because I was laughing so much.

'He's fucken flutered,' Hegarty told them and that quickly became the joke at which we all laughed.

Whenever I try to think about the walk back that night my thoughts rush headlong to what happened when we arrived. Only for one single moment will they slow down, impeded in their stampede forward by an image of Hegarty lying down in the middle of the road in a bunched up position which he said would guarantee his survival if a car came. Threatening to put it to the test because I said I did not believe him he stayed there waiting. I listened for the sound of an engine and several times imagined I heard one. Each time I waited, imagining the high black hedge filling with light – its dense tracery webbing the road and illuminating the scene for a second before Hegarty got mangled. And I waited, vaguely thinking that I might suddenly hear crows clamouring above, screeching as they had on the day he fell from the upper storey in the castle. But the only sound in the vast crispy stillness was the unbroken trickle of water somewhere deep inside the black hedge.

We sat down on the embankment opposite our house. The plan to stay in it had been abandoned after my father pulled out the sinks, leaving it even less habitable than it had been when we arrived. I kept hoping Hegarty would say something about it because I did not want him just sitting there feeling sorry for me. He stood up and walked over, squeezed through the door and disappeared inside. I followed, and hearing his steps above me, went straight up to my room where I found him leaning on the sill looking out across the green. I had just about settled into the narrow space beside him when he swung around and in a voice full of urgency told me to wait exactly where I was for a minute. He was gone before I could ask why.

I looked out, watching the shadows move across the green, spreading layers of darkness in quick succession. I peered into the dense blackness left in their trail as they swept evenly over the big spindling tree, blotting it out. As Moratorium Row disappeared into the fathomless darkness, I thought I saw a figure moving between the wrapped statues. But the shadowy pockets of light around those dim figures were absorbed into the darkness at such a rate that I could not be sure.

When Hegarty came back I asked him if he had been over

there, but he was so intent on giving instructions that he didn't even consider the question.

'You go over and keep a lookout,' he said, pointing at the big tree. 'And keep well out of sight, if you see anyone coming just stay put, cough, don't fucken come down, I'll be down at the statues. As soon as I have the job done I'll be up to you.'

He handed me the paraffin drum he had brought back with him. Taking his ace of diamonds lighter out of his pocket, he flicked the top off. As he turned it upside down he gestured to me to tip the drum up and pour some oil into the small opening. I was concentrating on trying to hold the drum steady when, speaking in a half-whisper he said, 'I gave 'em a gallon each so there isn't much left.'

The paraffin spilled out onto his hand and dripped onto the floor. I felt a bolt of raw excitement shoot through me as the fumes filled the room. I went ahead, crouching down behind Moratorium Row, slowly edging my way through darkness so dense that until I actually stepped forward it seemed impenetrable. When I came to the scaffolding I stopped. In the cold night air the smell of paraffin was sharp, somehow more distinct than it had been inside. I prodded the plastic covering on the statues to gauge the depth of the protective straw underneath. My finger sank right in, going much further than I expected and as the soggy straw gave way I felt another wave of excitement. I decided not to go onto the green at that point but to creep up towards the big tree on the moor side of the wall and then dash across if the coast was clear.

Everything about the wall was familiar. The barkish texture of the lichen left a pocked imprint on the palms of my hands as I climbed over. It was a sensation I knew in such a particular way that the two years or so since I climbed over that wall burst into nothingness – like a bubble – as my memory collided with the event itself. And I ran towards the tree fully convinced that I was reclaiming something that I had come to believe was irretrievable. I stood behind the tree, inhaling the biscuity, fungus-like smell. In that instant, my world lit up beyond all expectation by a flame erupting so high into the night sky that for a while it seemed unconnected with anything on the ground. And it burned up there, well above the statues, shooting down every few seconds to feed on its source and then instantly flaring up again. With each soaring leap my excitement turned to terror, rising and falling in such quick succession that I felt both terrified and wildly excited at the same time. But I knew while I watched that I was not wholly lost to terror or excitement. I believed, though not very confidently, that I would not regret being there.

I heard one of the statues crack and watched as the remaining straw fell away in clouds of sparkling dust, creating new pockets of fire on the ground which burned out as fast as they started. I kept thinking that Hegarty was going to arrive at the tree as he said he would, but there was no sign of him. I waited for about fifteen minutes after the fire had died down and then left, thinking that when he saw how big the fire was he had decided not to stick around.

When I got in, I found Agnes and Gretta asleep on the couch. They were both sitting up, leaning towards different ends of the couch, still in their dancing costumes. Without having to think too much about it I guessed that there had been a row with Queenie and probably a whole lot more besides. I sank into the nearest chair, an armchair with a mauve and cream crocheted cushion, and fell asleep.

When I woke, in what felt like a few minutes though it was several hours, Bríd was standing over me, looking down as if I was coming to after an accident. And when I went to speak the inside of my mouth was so parched that no words came. I discovered the full extent of my thirst when I tried to swallow, looking at Bríd who was speaking to me as if there was nothing wrong.

'You better get a move on, the hackney car will be here in

a minute, your father went to get it over an hour ago. We're going back.'

I did not need to ask why we were leaving two days earlier than planned and Bríd did not feel the need to explain either. It marked a return to a way of doing things which was easy and familiar.

All our luggage was ready and waiting in the hall and when my father came back with the hackney car, Bríd brought it as far as the door for him to collect. He took most of it in one go, throwing it carelessly into the open boot. Nobody spoke the whole way to the station and the hackney man entered into the mood, driving slowly and looking straight ahead like an undertaker.

As we drove past our house with the half-open door and the wigless heads toppled to one side, I felt relieved at being able to write it all off with such ease. I glanced in the opposite direction, hoping that the others would continue looking at our house and would not see the statues. The one which had cracked in the fire had split from crown to crotch. One of the halves had tilted in the direction of the other statue, resting against it shoulder to shoulder.

The boat train was not due for several hours but after about twenty minutes a train made an unscheduled stop and we got on, prepared to get off again two stations up the line to wait there instead.

As the train pulled out I heard someone shouting and before I had fully registered that it was Hegarty's voice, I saw him running along the platform in long leaping strides. He must have seen us when we paused at Singleton's. And he kept pace with the train, all the time keeping his arms stretched out, his fists tightly closed and his thumbs up. His face was full of triumph.

13

I leaned against the deck rails, looking at the froth tailing the whole way back to the pier. I wanted to believe that in the grand scale of things, the time I spent watching the coastline growing distant was somehow significant. But I felt nothing much, except a mild sense of relief. I tried to charge the occasion with importance by saying something out loud, something that would sound final, like 'that's that' or 'well'. But it didn't work. Nothing I did or thought gave the journey any significance beyond itself. So I just watched the fragile wisps of light holding the coastline together as they flickered into tiny specks.

My attempts to make the departure mean something reminded me of the way I felt when my grandmother died. I kept looking at her during the wake, repeating to myself, 'she's dead', trying to make myself feel like I thought I ought to feel. It's not that I found it difficult to accept. Not at all. For months before she died her approaching death had loomed larger than her life and so when she actually died it just became official. I felt the same way as I watched the coastline disappear, a sense that, for the most part, beginnings and ends are well under way before they become apparent. That end I was trying to conjure up as I watched the coastlights fading was already well settled into the past.

I went below deck to the bar where my father stood with four or five men. Bríd and my sisters were sitting at a white formica table nearby. As I approached, Bríd stood up and asked me to mind her seat while she went to the shop on the upper deck to buy a memento. I sat down, thinking about the hundreds of souvenir colleens and leprechauns on the high sills of the Club. My father took off his coat and as he did I saw that he was wearing the freedom medal. I wondered if he had been wearing it all day. The other men looked at it and one or two of them made little gestures of admiration, a tilt of the head, a glass raised – that sort of thing. Their conversation about the condition of the roads in Ireland smouldered to a close and in the silence they looked, first at the medal and then at the floor. My father peered into his glass, concentrating like a clairvoyant. I think they were waiting for him to say something but it was clear to me that he would not speak first. But they waited, smacking their lips and licking the froth from around their mouths.

'See there was this woman.'

They all laughed and the man who had begun to tell the joke paused and started again.

'See there was this woman, the same one.'

They all laughed again, this time with more gusto.

'Big tits, she had big tits.' And he put his pint down, cupped his hands over his chest and extended the cups as far out as his hands would go.

'See, this big.'

The whole group rocked with laughter and one man, who was drinking a Club Orange, laughed so much that he had to purse his lips to hold in the mouthful of orange he had just taken.

'Her husband was a bit short-sighted, you know what I mean, short-sighted.'

He closed his eyes and started to grope the air about him, opening and closing his hands and then cupping them as he had done a few seconds before.

The group crumpled and some of them moved back to give more room to a man who was laughing so much that he had lost his balance. The punchline was drowned out by the laughter and all the falling about.

'What's the medal for?'

The man who told the joke had asked the question while the others were still laughing. And they continued laughing as they looked at the medal, repeating bits of the joke for each other, shaking their heads and taking turns to say 'that was a good one'.

My father set about answering but the joker was already telling another joke.

'There was this fella. Paddy Irishman. Turns to the fella beside him at the cinema and says, between you and me we have five balls. Fella turns to him and says, what do you mean? Have you only one?'

My father who had not laughed as much as the others at the first joke found this one very funny. Everyone did. With his eyes shut and his pint held close to his chest, he chuckled. But as he went to raise his pint, still chuckling a bit, the medal went straight in. He looked up. Nobody had seen what happened. And then for some unknown reason he purposefully drew their attention to it, leaving it there until everyone around had a good look before slowly lifting it out of the stout by the ribbon.

'I'll tell you this much,' he said, 'It's the first drink Dev and Cúchulain ever had together.'

Everyone, except the joker, laughed. And I laughed loudest,

so loud that my father turned around and looked at me. He looked at me for so long that I began to feel there was something peculiar about the way I was laughing. When I thought about the joke I realized that it wasn't all that funny, hardly funny at all. And still I felt like laughing, unable to see that what I was trying to do was mark the moment.

It occurred to me that the events of the previous few days might have led him to look less seriously on the past. But that possibility was short-lived because when Bríd came back he had to take his coat from the empty seat and as he leaned across I told her that while she was away Dev and Cúchulain had had a drink together. Nobody laughed, least of all my father who again looked at me with suspicion.

'Look what I got.'

From a bulging duty free bag, Bríd pulled out a large cellophane tube with a doll inside wearing a tartan dress and a white flouncy blouse. Its lips were curled up at the corners but its expression was clearly one of pain. When Bríd took it out of the cellophane tube one of its stiletto shoes came off and fell on the ground. Agnes got under the table to look for it. Gretta joined her and before she began searching, listed all the places it could be. Soon, directed by Gretta, we had to stand up from our seats.

'It's lost and we won't find it now,' Bríd said, but she continued to search, shaking the coats and moving the bags about. 'Anyway it shouldn't have been wearing shoes like that, not stilettoes.'

I picked up the cellophane tube and began to read the tag which was attached to the top with a little piece of tartan ribbon.

'Bonny Highland Lass.' I read it again just to make sure.

'It's a Scottish doll, look, it says it here, read it, Bonny Highland lass, Scotland's fairest and Scotland's finest.'

'Show me, give it to me. Here, give it to me.' Bríd was annoyed at her mistake, even more so when she realized that it could not be exchanged for a colleen because one of the shoes was lost. But her annoyance gave way to laughter, loud hearty laughter, when Gretta replaced the tartan skirt with one made from shredded beer mats. And we all laughed as Gretta guided the doll across the white formica table, mimicking the tones of a compere at a fashion show.

'... and the most fetching number in this year's spring collection is Moira's cardboard ensemble ...' making the doll slip on a stout spill, saying, 'Oops, a little accident. Moira has had a little accident.'

When we arrived back in the flat the following afternoon and Lil came down to ask how we got on, Bríd told her we'd had a marvellous time. And as she described it she laughed, sometimes uproariously, telling Lil things that made her shriek with laughter. She kept using the word holiday which until then none of us had used. And she added several bits that were not true, glancing over at me and tilting her head in Lil's direction as if to suggest that Lil was the one who was inventing things about the holiday. One of the things she told Lil was that when we got home there were cows in our house, correcting herself, after Lil had laughed a great deal, by saying that they were not actually in the house but probably had been, or might as well have been – it was in such a mess.

'It's true about some people living with cows in Ireland,' Lil replied when she had stopped laughing. 'Gus says he knew people who did.'

'It wouldn't surprise me, nothing would surprise me about the way people live over there. Look at my own sister Queenie, she doesn't even have an indoor toilet.'

Bríd hardly stopped to draw her breath as she rattled off all the ways in which things were backward at home, demolishing it all, every bit of it in a torrent of unreserved mockery. And they laughed and laughed until the smallest gesture from either left them both speechless with laughter.

When my father, who had gone out to get a paper, came

back, Bríd asked him to show the freedom medal to Lil. She wiped the tears of laughter from her eyes with her apron while he held it in front of her, dangling it as Dineen had on the day of the commemoration ceremony.

'Get Gus,' she said to me. 'He'd love to ...' and before she could say 'see it', she had covered her mouth with her hand, bursting into a new bout of laughter. Breathless, she tried to explain to my father what she was laughing at by pointing at Bríd and saying, 'cows in the toilet.'

Gus came down straight away.

'It's worth a few bob,' he said examining the medal closely. 'How much depends, of course, on whether it's plate or not. If it's plate, then not that much, but if it's the real thing it could fetch a pretty penny.'

Gus was an expert on a whole range of topics, frequently behaving like one when no expertise was required. He weighed up everything that was said – even offhand observations about the weather – and responded, nodding a little before he delivered his judgement. My father found this irritating and often, after we had taken a lift home from the Club with Gus and Lil, he would shake his head and say that Gus had far too much to say for himself.

I could see that same irritation mount as Gus held the medal close to his face and scratched it with a straight pin he had taken from behind his jacket collar.

'Plate, I'm afraid. Thought so at first. Mind you, it's quite a heavy plate but it's still not worth much. If you want to have it valued I know a bloke. Do it for free, he would.'

It should have been clear to Gus from the way my father took the medal back that he did not want to have it valued. But Gus, who never paid any attention to anyone, continued to ply my father with advice and information.

'Good quality plate is worth a lot more than it used to be. Time was when nobody wanted it. But all that has changed now. And another thing, that medal, you know it could become a collector's item.'

'It's not for sale,' my father said gruffly and it was clear, even to Gus, that the conversation was at an end.

I never saw the medal again, at least not until years later – after my father died. It was stored away with all the other things that pointed to the world we had left, a world we talked about less and less. Whenever we did, it was almost always in fun; light-hearted jokes about how primitive things were at home. My father's efforts to stop us were not only unsuccessful, but he often became the butt of our jokes as well. Led by Gretta, we mocked his accent under our breaths and when, during the summer after that first trip home, England began to emerge as World Cup favourites we purposefully taunted him, asking each other who *we* were playing next. What were *our* chances? If my father did not react then Gretta would repeat the question pausing before and after the words 'we' and 'our'. Watching the English matches turned into an elaborate game during which we not only demonstrated our eagerness to support England but dramatized it out of all proportion. Gretta screamed with delight every time England took possession of the ball and threw herself over the back of the couch if there was a free kick or a corner awarded against England. During the final against Germany she took to jumping up and running around the flat shouting 'Oh no, oh no, oh God no' whenever there was the slightest setback for England. When victory finally came we all went berserk, wildly flaunting our excitement. As well as being a national victory it was, for us, a personal victory. My father just sat there looking at the crowds milling around the victorious team.

When, a few years later, the bombing campaign in Northern Ireland began, he sat in that same bewildered silence, listening to us saying things like, 'vicious bloodthirsty savages' or 'twisted psychopathic sadists'. Once, just after I arrived back from my first term in teacher training college, we were looking at a television report on an IRA bombing. He said something about freedom but he said it with such little conviction that it almost failed to become a full phrase. Was it a question? I would like to think it was. I would like to think that the events of his own life led him to doubt some of the beliefs which left him so much at odds with the world in which he lived. But I did not respond, sensing that the question, if it was a question, would once again lead us back to those events of his early life. It was probably just as well that I did not respond because I was then every bit as lost in a sea of love, peace and happiness as he was in his illusory freedom.

During the summer that followed, London seemed to be the epicentre of changes vibrating around the globe from the Himalayas to San Francisco. In mid July my father, Bríd and Agnes went on holiday to Ireland with the Finnegans. Gretta and I waved goodbye to them, hardly able to wait for that caravan with its yellow number plate and GB sticker to disappear. I had asked some blokes from my class down to London for a few days. It began as a plan for three of us to go and see *Hair* but it ended up as a group of eleven staying in the flat for ten days.

Gretta brought home an assortment of people she met at work. She called it work, affecting the blasé manner of someone much older. It was, in fact, an unpaid summer job minding a bric-à-brac stall on Petticoat Lane for an hour every lunchtime. There, among posters of Che Guevara and the Maharishi, rainbow candles, tie dyed T-shirts, psychedelic scarves, Indian beads and joss sticks, she smiled at the passersby. If she thought any of the people who stopped to browse looked a bit lost or aimless she invited them to the flat, American backpackers, buskers, au pairs running away from what Gretta called slavery in Weybridge and Hampstead. She invited them all. She had become a vegetarian and spent most of the afternoons making large quantities of couscous which she served in brown pottery bowls. Sitting on the floor in the flat, surrounded by backpacks and guitars, we all nodded, whispering extended *wows* as the chilli peppers burned right through the roofs of our mouths.

When Bríd and my father arrived home there was little or no evidence of what had gone on while they were away, except for our attempts to cover it up, the most evident of which was the sickly smell of pine-scented disinfectant, poured all over the flat as the caravan drew up outside. But the sitting tenant on the top floor confided in Lil, who promptly told Bríd, that there had been a love-in in our flat while they were all away, 'with foreign looking people smoking reefers on the front door steps all day long'.

Bríd challenged Gretta and me and, although I was very flattered by Mr Whistler's description of what had been going on, I denied the accusation. Bríd was willing enough to believe me, mainly because she didn't like Mr Whistler. But Gretta would not answer any of Bríd's questions unless she called her by the new name, Vanessa, assumed while they were on holiday.

As that summer went on – long hot London days – the sense of possibility that marked its arrival became more and more intense. There were times – and not just at the big open air concerts in the parks – when it seemed certain that the old order, 'that cold, faceless society', as we referred to it, had given way to a new era of concern and involvement. I felt that I was surfing in on the swell of that great wave, sharing the vision of a new world order with a generation, every bit as hopeful as me. There was no voice in the background whispering caution, no one pointing out that each new generation fixes on an ideology of hope which carries it forward and certainly no one, least of all me, prepared to see that my father had had a summer of optimism once – which, despite the odds, he was unwilling to forget.

Before she went back to school that September, Gretta changed her name again, this time to Wanita. We laughed a lot about it, pronouncing it with a honky Bronx accent. But it was only the beginning of a series of attempts she made to invent a new persona for herself. These attempts, which included eighteen months as a cook in the Orani Orishana Temple in Putney, went on for years – until finally, aged twenty-three, she began a pre-diploma art course in a progressive Poly. It was a new beginning and Bríd and Agnes, who fretted endlessly about Gretta's welfare, made a point of going to the end of year exhibition to see Gretta's work. They were so outraged by what they saw that I decided to go and see it a few days later.

Each student had been given a space, a cubicle about twice the size of a telephone booth. 'Every potential artist,' said a leaflet explaining the project, 'must discover themselves before they set about interpreting the world and their experiences of it.' That seemed straightforward enough.

The entrance to Gretta's booth was through a hula-hoop from which pinkish-purplish tissue paper had been stretched to cover the whole front of the booth. Gretta, who had recently resumed her original name, sat chained to the opposite wall. The chain was made up of large colourful playschool Xs and Ys, ordered into the pattern of a female chromosome chain. It was not long enough to allow her full entry into her booth which the director enthusiastically told me and one or two others who were standing about, was a statement of frustration on behalf of all women who were unable to enter fully into their own lives.

Inside the booth a pale blue light illuminated a collage of cut outs, bits of clothing, photographs – all sorts of things. I was hard put to understand the significance of a lot of them: a flattened thimble nailed to the thumb of a plastic glove, a game titled snakes and ladders with no snakes and no ladders on the hand-painted gameboard, a bucket of broken glass.

On the other hand, some of the things, like the collage of wildly obscene magazine cutouts, were clearly designed to shock and had an immediate impact. Two pieces were familiar and when I spotted them I laughed loudly. One was a Mandy doll dressed in an Irish dancing costume with several feathered voodoo pins stuck into her temples. The other was a statue of the Child of Prague with flashing red lights inserted into the eye sockets and a button at the base which said 'Please Press'. When I did, the booth filled with the sound of children's voices set against a heavy background hum. But amusement rapidly gave way to a disturbing feeling as I realized I was listening to a recording, familiar from television, of children at a feeding station in one of the East African famine areas. The low wail of a parched child's voice rose against the background murmur of women, fading over the next three or four minutes to a faint, single scratch of a voice before thinning out into nothingness.

I wanted to leave the booth and tell Gretta how over the top I thought the whole thing was, but some people had gathered around her and, full of excitement, the course director was pointing out the significance of the big Xs and Ys.

Then, without warning, Gretta leapt in the direction of the booth. She fell short of the entrance and lay in her jailbird leotard, dramatizing the confining effects of her gender chains.

At this point I left the booth and waited while the two people with the course director took notes and asked Gretta questions which she answered in a broad brogue, an accent so pronounced that it was impossible to follow what she was saying. She glanced across at me mischievously, while the course director interpreted what she said for the small audience. When they went into the booth she asked me, in a conspiratorial whisper, not to say anything until they had left.

I sauntered down to look at the other exhibits, uncomfortable with the timid smiles of the people sitting like fortune tellers outside their booths. The exotic, disturbing lives depicted inside were, for the most part, impossible to connect with the lifeless people sitting stoop-shouldered at each entrance.

'What was that all about?' I said to Gretta as I walked back up to her booth.

'Shush ... keep your voice down,' she hissed. She did not continue until the course director and the others were at the end of the long corridor leading to the front entrance. 'Those two men were from *Expression*, if they do an article on me, I'm certain to get a touring grant. Ian said so.'

'Why did you speak to them in that gobbledygook?'

'It helps if you're Irish, you know, all that spirit, more interesting, unpredictable, art, more ... ' she shrugged her shoulders and smirked. 'May as well cash in on it?'

But she was uneasy with her cynicism and was visibly looking for reassurance. When I did not provide it straight away she set about steering the conversation in a different direction. Pointing down the room to the other booths she raised her eyes and said, 'I'm bloody well not going to end up like those goons.'

I looked down at the wan faces, the neat composures, and I nodded. But that was not enough for Gretta, whose flashy anger was shooting up the scale.

'Makes me sick the way they troop up here and plod about looking at my work saying 'Fack' every ten seconds, like battery chickens. And you,' turning abruptly to me, 'You're out there thinking you're going to save the world teaching in that school for rejects. Pathetic. You'd do a bloody sight more for the human race if you told this lot the truth about themselves and their lousy work.'

Then, just as I was about to reply, she cut back in, 'They already know what I think.' And she yelled down the room 'Don't you,' and under her breath added, 'Pack of goons.'

Gretta got the travelling grant and spent that summer in her gender chains, leaping towards her booth in venues in and around London. She went on to become a successful performance artist whose best known show, 'Éire's Torn Soul', was described by one national newspaper as 'giving an unparalleled insight into the tormented psyche of Ireland'.

Gretta's attitude to this type of response, and to her performances in general, provided endless laughter whenever we met. She mercilessly mimicked people who took her performances seriously and the send-ups she did of their earnest questions were better than any of her public shows. Then, to everyone's surprise, except of course Gretta's, Felix her son was born. And true to his name, with his big mop of black Caribbean curls, he rapidly eroded her cynicism and like a singer who suddenly loses pitch, she backed out of the limelight and off the stage.

part three

14

Like a lot of people's plans, our plan to return to live in Ireland was tied up with a longing to return to the lives we had left. Although I had become aware of the impossibility of doing this during our first holiday home, I still did not abandon the idea. It became a refuge, somewhere to retreat to whenever I could not, or would not, take on the world about me. But I felt that I might damage, or even destroy, that refuge by going back on holiday. And whenever I did go I always felt the same sense of relief when leaving to return to London. It marked the end of days of conflict between the place as I imagined it and the place as it presented itself.

Gretta refused outright to go and ever since that first holiday has never been back. But my father and Bríd, despite her jokes about how primitive things were there, continued to look forward to returning permanently. They didn't say so but it was something we assumed was inevitable.

The flat we moved into on the last Sunday in September in

1963 was, despite all the talk about going home, the place where the greater part of our lives together took place. The temporary feeling which it had taken on during those early years lingered, as the presence of a former owner often lingers in a house long after a new one has moved in. It wasn't particularly evident in the immediate appearance of the place which, though dark, was comfortable in a plain sort of way. A standard lamp, with a pleated wine shade, cast a warm pinkish light over the three piece leatherette suite – the couch slightly angled to face the television. Set into the fawn tiled fireplace was an electric fire, a Fireglo which illuminated the hearth with varying shades of reddish orange light. On the mantelshelf above, between two blue vases, was the picture taken by Monsignor Mullen outside the Canon's house. Everything had remained in precisely the same position as the day we arrived. Nobody had taken possession of the flat by changing things around or getting new furniture. The fish tank which I got when my 'O' level results indicated that I was not going to be a blue collar worker was about the only thing that could not be put into a bag and carried away by hand.

There would have been no difficulty getting a place of our own, a council flat, bigger and a lot less expensive. But there was never any question of my father or Bríd applying, just as there was never any question of them registering to vote or taking any steps which might make us feel a sense of permanence.

My father and Bríd's plan to return began to take definite shape as her retirement date approached. The actual date, August 1979, became a fixture when the butcher's shop where she was cashier was taken over by a company which ran a chain of butcher shops in south London. Special pension entitlements were made for Nick and Bert, the assistant butchers – and Bríd – so that they would stay on and the shop would not lose established trade.

She and Lil talked about the takeover endlessly. Mr Rupton's changes of mind were reported in detail to Lil, who, when she heard about the pension entitlements, had great difficulty in hiding her resentment. In this way we all came to know the details of the scheme, assuming all along that when it came to pass Bríd and my father would be returning to live in Ireland.

But when the time came she did not retire. There were always reasons why she could not leave at any particular point. Sets of accounts to be produced which a new cashier couldn't possibly be expected to deal with and staff she was keeping an eye on for Mr Rupton whose sciatica kept him from work for long periods.

My father had retired from his job at the tannery three years before. And for the period while Bríd worked towards her pension he got a part-time job as a groundsman in a boating club, way out past Staines. As her retirement approached he set about organizing the renovation of our old house, going over for a week in March of that year to get things under way. But despite an undertaking by the builder, Dinny Hardiman, to start work the day after my father went back, it did not begin until the following September.

From the word go there were difficulties, some of which my father thought he got sorted out on a second trip home later that year. But soon afterwards the work – and there was very little done – stopped again. When, after weeks of unsuccessful phone calls, he tracked Hardiman down, he was bluntly told that he would be better off getting the house knocked down and building a new one in its place.

My father stubbornly resisted this suggestion. His impenetrable gloom hung over everything that winter and did not lift until plans for a new house, reluctantly agreed to, were at an advanced stage. To save on the expense of having the old one knocked down and cleared away, they asked Queenie for a site in the small field to the right of her house. She was very much looking forward to Bríd's return and without a moment's hesitation, gave them the whole field. The building of a three bedroomed modern bungalow was finally about to begin when, out of the blue, it changed to become what Bríd called 'a luxurious extension' to Queenie's house.

When I first heard this, on one of my infrequent visits back to the flat, I was very surprised. I looked across to my father, certain that he would need no encouragement to say how he felt about living with Queenie. But he glanced at Bríd who started telling me how lonely it could be in the winter without a soul to talk to. I could not imagine how they had agreed on such a daft idea.

'Besides,' Bríd said confidentially, as if there was someone eavesdropping, 'Queenie needs help, she has difficulty getting around and when you think about it, who else has she?'

She continued to pick her words cautiously and I recognized for the first time her reluctance to return to Ireland. A luxurious extension to Queenie's house, as she kept calling it, was a compromise, something my father must have agreed to, or maybe even suggested, to overcome that reluctance. However they had arrived at the arrangement, they made it clear that they didn't want to hear what I thought about it. But I couldn't sit there ignoring what would, without doubt, turn out to be disastrous.

I thought of the time when Queenie had come over for a hip replacement on the National Health and had stayed in the flat for six weeks. Even Agnes, whose patience was legendary, moved in with Gretta until Queenie went back. Then I remembered the first holiday home. Straight away, so many other collisions with her came to mind that I was at a loss to know which one to remind them of first. Bríd stood up and with her voice full of reassurance said, 'There'll be adjoining doors, we'll have to knock, just like a house, if we want to see each other.'

I looked at the plates on the table, the remains of lunch –

semicircles of grizzly fat caked in gravy, little heaps of salt sodden with the reddish brown juice of the beef, a few peas pushed to the side. I was determined to point out the foolishness of the plan. But that determination just started to drain away in the face of their unity – the way they sat, the comfort in which they ignored each other and their unquestioning loyalty to each other.

My father and I waited in silence until Bríd returned a few minutes later carrying three bowls of ice cream with wafers sticking up like wings. Suddenly it was as if, sedated by all that was familiar, I had become a child again, sitting there between them scooping up the Walls Neapolitan Ice Cream: my favourite.

The following Wednesday evening my father went out to buy a paper and, if it had been summer, Bríd would not have been concerned when, an hour later, he was still out. Sometimes in fine weather he would go to the newsagents at the other end of the High Street, sauntering up and back, looking in shop windows. But it was a bitterly cold February evening and the window of my flat was already opaque with fans of overlapping frost when Bríd rang. At first I thought that he had gone home, that he had suddenly come to his senses and realized how doomed the extension plan was. He was on his way to call a halt to the scheme before anything got under way. I was so convinced of this that I began to point out to Bríd all the pitfalls of moving in with Queenie, all the things I had failed to say the previous Sunday and which had been coursing through my head ever since. She listened for a while. But then, like children who have waded too far into an imaginary world, our conversations came to a standstill.

When I had put the receiver down I knew that the instant I described his decision as 'spur of the moment', we both began to doubt that he was on his way home. The phrase sank like an anchor. Bríd repeated it several times trying to make it apply to him. But it did not and could not. We were left with little to say to each other except that we would be in touch later that night.

'He might,' I said as I was about to hang up, 'arrive at the front door just as you put down the receiver.'

Grasping at every possibility, she asked me to hold on while she checked.

She was gone for about ten minutes and as the time went by I imagined that he had arrived back and she was so relieved that she had forgotten I was at the other end of the line.

'No sign, I went down as far as the corner, it's freezing, no sign, there's hardly anyone about, it's so cold.'

As soon as I put down the phone it occurred to me that I should have offered to go round so I rang Bríd back to tell her I was on my way.

She answered, full of expectation, impatient when she heard me speak. Then continuing in a hesitant, distracted voice she told me that Agnes was on her way and she'd know what to do. They would, she said, 'keep in touch'.

Agnes had moved back to live in the flat about a year before when she had completed her three year nursing course. If my father ever came close to thinking that bringing us up in England had worked out well, then it was on the day Agnes got her SRN certificate. I wasn't there for the presentation but went along to the Club in the evening where Bríd had said she hoped we could all meet. My father, clutching a fistful of notes, was buying drinks for everyone he knew. He pointed to Agnes from the bar and she smiled, both pleased and embarrassed at the same time. Anyone looking down the room from the bar would have had little difficulty identifying Agnes as his daughter. It wasn't so much the obvious – the shock of crinkly sand-coloured hair and the broad face, with eyes lost in a gather of lines, all scrunched up as though visibility was poor. What made them so similar was their shyness. Their heads were nearly always tilted to the right and both had this stark expression that was both trusting and defiant at the same time. Even their movements were similar – self conscious to the point of often appearing awkward. The similarities, and Agnes's age – she was only eight when we came to live in England – led him to regard her, in some ways, as more wholly his child than Gretta or me. He did not indulge Agnes, so it wasn't favouritism in that sense. It was what Bríd called 'a way they had with each other', something that looked like tolerance but which, by the time she was in her early teens, was unmistakably affection. Gretta, who had always been inseparable from Agnes, retaliated by becoming openly hostile. She remained so right up until Agnes left to begin her nursing course, always making a point of excluding her from anything that was going on – mimicking her when she thought nobody was listening. Even after she had left, Gretta continued to taunt Agnes. She mocked the meticulous way Agnes went about things and joked endlessly about the charm bracelet for which Agnes bought a gold charm every second month. So when Gretta arrived in the Club that evening, everyone was pleased. Felix was only a few weeks old and asleep in a papoose with Gretta's jacket zipped right up to the back of his head.

Lil and Gus came along later and Gus took lots of photographs. The one he took of Felix showing his distaste for the drop of Guinness which Gretta fed him from the tip of her finger is still pinned up in the middle of all the post cards behind the Club bar.

I waited until I was sure that Agnes was in before I rang the flat and while I waited for one of them to answer I tried to anticipate the news. The phone went on ringing for so long that I dialled again.

When Agnes finally answered she asked me to hold on because 'Mum' – as she had taken to calling Bríd – 'is very upset.' I called after her as she put the receiver down, sure that there must have been some definite news. But there wasn't. Gus and Lil had come down and Gus had gone into the Club – the phone had been engaged all evening – to see if my father was there. It was unlikely. He had left his wallet in the flat and could only have had some loose change with him.

'How much was' and before I had even said, 'in the wallet', I realized how irrelevant the question was. Agnes, accepting, without knowing why, that this was in some way significant, said she would go and check. Any vague interest I had in the answer disappeared as the memory of a man standing at the public telephone in the Club came into sharp focus. When I first saw him, and it had all happened years before, I thought he had been beaten up because his lips were swollen and his nostrils dilated. I had often seen him sitting by himself reading *The Limerick Leader*. He always nodded when he saw us and smiled – a burly beam of a smile that lingered. Later on Lil told us that the man's daughter had died that morning. Everyone listening drew back from her, and I waited, certain that one of them, probably Bríd, would ask how she had died. They didn't. It was as if they all knew. Then Lil nodded. As soon as I got the chance I asked Bríd what had happened and in a very matter-of-fact way she said meningitis.

In the crisscross way thoughts get tangled, I imagined that at that very moment my father was standing by the public telephone in the Club waiting for a call.

'Nine pounds.'

'Maybe he had some more with him. Look, I think I'll come down.'

'There's not much point. It's almost midnight. I'm going to give Mum a sleeping pill. I'll just wait till Gus gets back – see if Dad turned up at the Club. I'll ring if things change. OK?' And when I agreed: 'Ta-ra.'

I had known that Agnes would take control in a practical way, but was surprised and maybe a bit uneasy about the extent to which she did. She gave the impression that it was more her concern than anyone else's.

Of all the possibilities the one that preoccupied me most,

as I drifted into sleep, was the idea that he might have run away to set up a completely separate life. I had seen a TV programme a few months before about people who just walk away from their families and cannot be traced. If the family go to the police and the person is located the police are obliged to keep that location secret if the person so wishes. When I woke, the idea was still lingering, but retreated when I thought about him and his age, 73, and the sort of things I knew he was – and wasn't – capable of doing. Then while I was shaving I realized that in my fantasy I was the one talking to the police, telling them that I did not want to be contacted by any members of my family.

When I rang that morning Agnes was fully convinced that he was on his way to Ireland, which she kept pronouncing without the 'r'. Queenie had been contacted and had promised to meet him off the afternoon train. It was all arranged, only a question of time before the whole thing got sorted out. Unsure of what to think and swayed by Agnes's conviction, I went along with it, pointing out, as the conversation came to a close, that it had been my first response the night before.

On my way to work, I thought about Queenie standing on the platform waiting to meet my father off the afternoon train. It was difficult to imagine how he would go about telling her that the extension was off. I wondered if there would be a scene. While I thought about them I cast Queenie in the trouble-making role, the one who had to be challenged. It was, I suppose, easier than accepting that Bríd's reluctance to return to live in Ireland was at the centre of whatever was going on.

I had built up such a clear image of their meeting, every detail of it, that when I heard he was not on the afternoon train I had difficulty believing it. I knew then that the only option left was to contact the police. But Bríd, wary of any official involvement, resisted all attempts we made to get her to the police station. She kept saying he would turn up and asked us several times to imagine what his reaction would be when he heard that we had been to the police. She sat on the edge of the couch telling us about the time when she did not hear from him for two weeks. The money, wired back to us in Ireland from the post office near the Club every Friday, did not arrive. As she pieced the story together she lost concentration, glancing about, standing up to do things, telling us what it was like when there was no money.

By nine that night I had given up trying to persuade her. Then she changed her mind. She did not explain why and before we were sure of what was happening she had put on her best coat and hat, full of purpose. Agnes, until then in charge, was suddenly trailing behind, adjusting to the turn things had taken.

I filled out a missing person's form and gave it to the policeman who glanced over it as he went back to get the half-smoked cigarette he had left burning on the edge of the high shelf behind the counter. He drew heavily on the cigarette, exhaling the smoke in a big gush, before he came over and handed the form back.

'We haven't got a missing person here.' He was much friendlier than I thought he would be. 'Twenty-four hours isn't enough. What identification did he have on him?'

'None, at least none that we know if, just went out to get a paper, didn't even bring his wallet with him and. . . .' Agnes stopped to draw breath.

'Have you checked the hospitals?'

I looked at Agnes, who was holding her breath, unsure whether she should answer the policeman's question or continue with what she had been about to say.

'With no identification . . . and his age, it's just a possibility, best be certain.'

'He's in the best of health.' Bríd spoke so loudly that a policewoman typing at the back of the room looked up to see what was going on.

'What we do is hang onto the form, save you filling it in again if he doesn't turn up. By the way, has your husband ... Mr ...' and he looked at the form, searching for the name, 'gone missing before?'

Then, clearly something occurred to him about us or about my father, some possibility that made him much more formal in his approach.

'Has the missing man ever been in police custody?'

As I shook my head – and we all shook our heads vigorously – I thought of the freedom medal and the commemoration ceremony, all the flags and the bunting and of how proud I was.

Suddenly I was torn between an inclination to explain, maybe even apologize, and a surging anger which was only containable because I did not know who or what I was angry with.

The policeman, half-listening to our over-anxious defence of my father, went back to speak with the policewoman. She let her fingers rest on the keys while he stooped down over her, whispering, one hand resting on the edge of her desk, the other on the back of her chair.

'I told you we shouldn't have come down here.' Bríd's lips were firmly pressed together and she was looking directly at me.

When the policeman came back he checked every detail of the missing person's form again, calling me 'Sir' whenever he asked me a question. He then went into an adjoining room. We stood there waiting until, after about ten minutes, the policewoman followed him in. When she reappeared she walked straight to her desk, sat down and, glancing briefly in our direction, told us we were free to go.

'I told you it would be no use coming here. And there's no telling what he'll have to say about it when he gets back.'

I wasn't sure which of us Bríd was speaking to, she was a few steps ahead and didn't turn around when she spoke. But despite what she said about going to the police, it was clear from the confident way she spoke that she was relieved to discover that my father was not officially missing.

When we got back to the flat Agnes began ringing the big hospitals. As one admissions office after another reported no unidentified admissions, Bríd's confidence grew. The first hospital Agnes rang was the one she worked in herself and when she had rung all the others she decided to ring back and ask the matron what steps she should take now that we were sure he had not been admitted anywhere. In that brief moment I was imagining that there might be other places, special places, where unidentified people could be brought if they were suddenly taken ill on the street. Before I could properly consider it, Agnes said the word morgue. She pronounced it slowly, drawing it out until it became a question that we all felt obliged to think about. Bríd's response was so immediate that neither Agnes nor I got a chance to consider the full implications of what the matron was suggesting. Bríd's hands began to shake and in between gulps of breath and compulsive sobs she complained of being cold. Agnes went to get a blanket and I sat listening while, over and over again, Bríd said he was dead. Nothing I said made any impact whatsoever. I'm not even sure she heard me asking questions, like how could she be so sure – questions that seemed feeble compared to the conviction with which she was pronouncing him dead.

Agnes brought back a red and yellow blanket which she carefully draped around Bríd's shoulders before she began leafing through the telephone directory. After about five minutes' searching, distracted throughout by Bríd's chant-like assertion that my father was dead, she rang directory enquiries.

Bríd's pallor changed as Agnes, covering the receiver mouthpiece, whispered that they give no detailed information by phone, but did confirm that there had been unidentified admissions within the previous twenty-four hours. If we wanted any more information we would have to go and formally declare our interest.

Agnes left to ask Lil if she would stay with Bríd while we went to the morgue but came back a few seconds later and said that maybe we ought to wait a day or two before taking such a drastic step.

'After all, he is only gone twenty-four hours.'

Bríd, until then strained and drawn by what she had been so quick to believe, lit up and, filled with hope at Agnes's suggestion, added 'not even officially missing yet.'

I was about to say that I felt certain we should go to the morgue, just to be sure that every possibility had been explored. But Bríd was so consoled and calmed by Agnes's plan to wait that I hesitated. In that moment of hesitation it occurred to me that if I agreed with them I could leave and, without saying anything, go to the morgue by myself.

Within an hour I learned that my father had had what was probably a mild heart attack and had dragged himself from the pavement into a doorway where some time during the night that followed he had died of hypothermia. It happened at the top of a small side street leading off the High Street, a corner where the entrance to a dry cleaners' opens onto both the High Street and the side street.

I have no memory of what he looked like when I identified him. Everything that happened from the moment I left the flat until I returned about two hours later seemed to become solidified into a single statement documenting the disturbing facts of his death. Any attempts I make to recall the circumstances under which I heard those facts fail. So sometimes, in between all the facts that surround his death and his burial, there is the irrational belief that he is still alive.

15

My father's death severed whatever threads of belonging I had held on to. Without him there could not be a complete regrouping, no moment when it would become clear that everything had, as Bríd used to say, worked out for the best.

Mingled with the grief I felt was a sense of loss for home which, during those early years in England, had been so skilfully avoided. It was as raw as it ever could have been, emerging from a tangle of deceptions which, during the days following my father's death, unravelled to reveal a grim picture of his life.

There was no question about where he would be buried. Before I began to make enquiries, it seemed like an enormously complicated task. But I quickly found out that there were undertakers specializing in Irish funerals. Instead of relief I felt rage, which I strained to control as I made the arrangements with a man from the undertakers, described by the receptionist a few minutes beforehand as an expert on Irish removals. From the way she spoke and kept repeating his name, Mr Coates, I had formed an image of an elderly, sombre man. But he turned out to be about twenty, twenty-two at most. I stared at him as he spoke, trying to contain my dislike for him by slotting him into one of the many general categories of English behaviour I had built up over the years. What a fake, a thick-headed schoolboy, not even a proper stuffed shirt, telling me that if I opted for a cremation ceremony in London first the overall cost would be considerably reduced. Everything he said, in his sniffling, rabbity East End accent was preceeded by, 'If I may suggest sir'. And no amount of generalizations about him and his type eased the frustration I felt in dealing with him. So, I effectively ended up saying yes to whichever of the options he happened to mention first, all except in the last case.

Would I 'wish to have the coffin accompanied on the boat?'

Brimming with impatience, I told him I – and several others – would be travelling with the coffin. I could hardly wait to sign the sheaf of forms he produced. But as the whole transaction came to an end, doors held open, understanding nods everywhere I looked, handshakes, I caught a glimpse of my own anger and left feeling exasperated.

The following evening we all met on the platform in Euston. By the time the train arrived we had drifted into groups which could have seemed unconnected to each other. Bríd, flanked by Lil and Agnes, had hardly said a word during the previous two days. Whenever anyone spoke to her Agnes answered and Bríd nodded. They stood furthest away from the edge of the platform, the only ones conspicuously in mourning. A few yards away, Gus and two men from the Club, Toddy Devoy and Ger Maguire, were gathered close together, all looking vacantly about the place and pitching the occasional word in my direction. I stood with Gretta and took turns with her holding Felix back from the platform edge. As soon as we got on the train he fell asleep, propped up on Gretta's lap with his head nestling into the cup of her arm. After a few whispered observations about how like my father she thought he was she gave in to the noise of the train. I stared out into the darkness, beginning to drift into sleep when I saw Gus's reflection in the glass. From the way he was rubbing his mouth with the palm of his hand, I knew he was on his way to the bar. With a slight head flick he asked me to join him, nodding down the aisle to where Devoy and Maguire waited until I stood up to go. After about an hour Lil joined us and in between each vodka and orange she drank – maybe six in all – she brought a cup of tea back to Bríd.

We arrived at one in the morning, about an hour before we could get on the boat. The station, a vast murky wasteland of empty platforms, had been tarted up since I last passed through. But the scheme to make it cheerful was clearly short-lived. Baskets of dried moss with stalks of dead geraniums falling over the sides swayed high up in the matrix of steel girders supporting the roof. The piped music, alternating with what sounded like a commentary on a horse race, could hardly be heard on the platform but was at peak volume in the cafeteria and the toilets. All around there were people asleep, slouching on benches – some still clutching polystyrene tumblers of greyish tea. In most of the corners and at the base of several of the big pillars lining the platforms there were people curled around suitcases.

Devoy and Maguire headed straight for the embarkation point. And as they quickstepped their way over and into the darkness Gus pointed at them, telling us that they intended to be first in the queue so as to line up the best seats in the bar for us all. He smiled at Bríd, expecting, I think, that she would be pleased but she only looked bewildered. Lil and Agnes, supporting her on both sides, guided her like an invalid over to the cafeteria.

We sat around waiting for the announcement. When it came, Gretta stood up and went over to where Bríd, Agnes and Lil were squeezed onto a two-seater bench. After saying something quietly to Agnes, she leaned across and said goodbye to Bríd. The ease with which Gretta was affectionate made all Agnes's care seem distant – almost institutional. Lil looked on in amazement, staring intently at Gretta as she walked over to where Gus and I were sitting. As she approached it occurred to me that neither Lil nor Gus were aware that Gretta had told us the evening before that she would only be coming as far as Holyhead. I turned to explain to Gus what was happening but all his attention was on Lil. Her arm was outstretched, reaching for Gretta, long before she got anywhere near her. Her last few steps were a sort of tumble in which she ended up catching Gretta by the elbow and digging her nails firmly into her arm. With her face pressed right up to Gretta's and her lips drawn into a straight line – turning what might have been a roar into a strained whisper – she said,

'What do you think you're doing?'

'I'm going back to London.'

Gretta's reply was contained and pleasant in a way that made me think she had not noticed the urgency with which Lil spoke.

'That's it,' Lil said without a moment's hesitation.' I've always known it. So have you,' she said, looking down at Gus. 'She's the selfish bitch we always thought she was.'

Gretta, intent on staying calm, glanced down at Felix and said nothing.

Then Lil, flustered by Gretta's composure, raised her voice.

'I've always known it. Everyone has – you're not satisfied enough with having disgraced your father with your carry-on when he was alive but you won't even bother to come to his funeral now – even for your mother's sake.'

Felix began to cry and Gretta, struggling to free herself from Lil's grasp, tried to pick him up. Angered by the persistence with which Lil held on to her, she drew back and in a cold, controlled voice said, 'Please, let go of my arm, Lil.'

When Lil let go, Gretta scooped up Felix and hiking him on to her hip tried to say goodbye to Gus who was making light of what had happened by smiling, shaking his head and in a resigned voice saying, 'Women,' over and over again. Lil was edging her way in beside him, sniffling as she pressed a starched white lace-edged handkerchief against her upper lip.

I had never seen Lil tear into somebody like that. But my view of what happened then changed over the next few days when it became apparent that my father's death had triggered a great deal more than the grief she might have been expected to feel. Most of the time it wasn't even grief, more a display of discontent which often bordered on hysteria and made the impact of my father's death not just sad but shocking. Lil and Gus had always seemed different to us. They were, like a lot of people I knew at the Club, thoroughly well settled into the life they had made for themselves in England. Their children Noe and Seamus, their grandchildren, their house, their caravan, were all fixtures in a world with which it was impossible to imagine them being at odds. Still, the further we travelled away from that world the more unrecognizable they became, accusing each other wildly and then comforting each other with unreserved compassion – swerving right off the tracks on which we had long since grown used to watching them glide smoothly.

During the early stages of the journey the boat swayed evenly, tilting from side to side at a pace I could anticipate. But it then began to heave and take sudden dips, throwing me forward and forcing me to hold onto the table with both hands. The vodkas Devoy and Maguire had bought for Lil before the bar closed slopped onto the table. The bar lights had been turned off except for the small inset bulbs directly above the tables and these were dimmed so low that everything, except the table tops, was in complete darkness. The only visible sign that anyone was awake was the hand –

Maguire's hand, maybe Devoy's – which every few minutes reached out from the darkness for one of the many pint glasses, through which they were working their way steadily.

'I don't understand it,' Agnes said to me the following morning as Devoy and Maguire left us to go to the train. 'They haven't stopped drinking all night and they look stone cold sober.'

We stood a little distance from the hearse into which my father's coffin had already been put by the Dublin undertakers, subcontracted to handle the Irish side of the funeral.

I was slow to reply to what Agnes said about Maguire and Devoy, anxious that I had failed to made adequate arrangements for the funeral.

'They'll probably head straight,' and as I said the words 'for the bar on the train', I could feel my attention straying to the hearse driver who was standing a few yards behind us. He had his hands clasped behind his back and was raising himself slightly by lifting his heels off the ground. Every minute or so he swayed forward very gently – and then back, balancing, with only the very front part of the soles of his shoes on the ground. I felt sure he was trying to make a point about having to wait. But it was difficult to know because, a few minutes earlier, when Gus had asked him if he would mind hanging on for a bit, he had said, 'Certainly,' and nodding his head added, 'I'm yours for the day.'

For a while I thought that not knowing where I stood with him had made me feel ill at ease. Then later, when the incident came to occupy a place in my thoughts out of all proportion to any interest I had in what that hearse driver did or thought, I realized that something quite different was going on. I was far too absorbed by all the other events of the day to see that on the basis of not knowing where I stood with him for that moment, I had quickly made a generalization about Ireland. It was the sort of observation that at one time I might have resented other people making, something along the lines of 'they never mean what they say' or 'you never really know what they're thinking'. The thought might have passed as quickly as it formed but it came to mark a shift in the way I looked at what I had been so reluctant to give up calling home.

I began to wish that Gus and Lil had not come with us. As soon as they heard there was no car arranged to follow the hearse, no funeral car, as they kept calling it, they had decided to go and hire a car. They did not speak directly to me, but well within my hearing asked each other and the hearse driver questions that were clearly meant to let me know how badly they thought I had handled things. As they left Lil turned to Bríd and full of reassurance said, 'Don't worry, don't worry one bit, we'll see to it that you won't have to take the train and be separated from him on his final journey.'

Bríd's face crumpled. I moved nearer, placing my arm lightly around her shoulder, afraid that she was going to faint. She was about to say something to me when Agnes whisked her over to sit on a wooden bench. There she handed her a turquoise and yellow capsule. Then, from her coat pocket, she took a small bottle of white lemonade, maybe it was water in a lemonade bottle, and held it up to Bríd's mouth, almost forcing her to drink it as Bríd struggled to swallow the capsule. Agnes said nothing to her, no instructions, no explanation, making it all seem routine. At the time I was too distracted by Gus and Lil and all the talk about the funeral car to make a connection between the turquoise and yellow capsule and the helpless way Bríd stumbled her way through those three bleak days.

When Gus and Lil came back about an hour later, they apologized to Bríd about the colour of the car. It was navy blue. They couldn't get a black one. Gus listed all the available colours – and makes – and might have gone on to engine size if Lil, tired of how stubbornly I resisted being drawn in, said, 'Anyway, it's better than being on the train,' then skittishly, 'which is where we could easily have ended up.'

The speed with which Lil recoiled from what she had said, and the frantic expression with which she appealed to Gus for protection, created the impression that she herself was frightened by how sour she had become. When Gus went to speak to the hearse driver about the route, Lil was at his heels with her head bowed, following like someone who could no longer trust their own judgement, someone who had placed themselves wholly in the care of another. Gus nodded as the hearse driver, pointing directly inland, gave instructions.

'I'll flash the lights,' Gus said smirking, 'if we want to stop.' And he threw his head back and tilted an imaginary glass towards his open mouth.

As it turned out we only stopped once, but we might have stopped several times if that first stop, a hotel outside Kildare, had gone well. It was very different to the sort of place that came to mind when Gus tilted that imaginary glass towards his mouth. But parking the hearse was not possible at any of the more likely places we looked at along the way.

As soon as Gus turned the engine off I leapt out of the car, anxious to order the drinks and so regain some of the ground I had lost by failing to arrange a funeral car.

'I'll have them sent down to you,' the barman said, gesturing to a room full of black formica tables.

I sank into one of the plush maroon window seats and waited. I tried to look through the curled glass of the 'olde curiosity' windows, wondering what was taking the others so long. The barman left the tray of drinks on the bar counter and pressed a button above the till. He then reached across to a silver coloured amplifier and by flicking one switch filled the lounge with a slow piano version of 'The Blue Danube'. It was less muted than the usual background music, a bit like the sound of a child playing with one finger. From a dark corner to my right a waitress walked into the bar throwing open the swing doors with such force that they opened and closed several times behind her, rhythmically drowning out the sound of the Blue Danube with a clang of saucepan noises. Inside, a frail old man carrying a big pot had stopped to look out at me and every time the doors opened he was standing in the exact same position, glaring with the worn-out look of a below deck captive.

The waitress slid the tray off the bar counter, sizing Gus up and down as he walked through from the reception area.

He gave me a thumbs up sign and leaned over the bar counter to say something to the barman. There was no response. Then Gus said something else, turned away, and walked down to where I was sitting. The barman, following his progress, shrugged his shoulders slightly – a gesture that seemed to indicate that he was not in a position to do whatever Gus had asked him.

'Ignorant bollocks,' Gus said, shaking his head and spreading his fingers to grasp the nearer of the two pints on the table in front of him.

'Where are the others?'

'Outside,' he said, sucking the head of the stout until it was no longer in any danger of spilling over the edge. 'They're not coming in, your mother said she couldn't sit inside with your father left out there.'

Between gulps, Gus licked his lips, explaining with less and less interest that the hearse driver, prompted by Bríd's reluctance to leave the hearse unaccompanied in the carpark, decided that it was his job to stay with it. Then waving his hand in the general direction of the carpark, Gus said, 'There's one of them worse than the next.' I gathered he was talking about Agnes and Lil who probably made a point of telling him that their place was with Bríd.

'And that bollocks,' Gus said, pointing directly at the barman, 'said no when I told him I was bringing the drinks out to the carpark.'

He poured half the pint I got for the hearse driver into my

glass and half into his own and while he was doing it asked me if I wanted the vodka, snapping it up and swallowing it before I answered. He did not wait while I paid and when I came out they were all packed into the car with the engine running, ready to go.

'That's the last we'll see of that place,' Gus announced as we waited for the hearse to drive out. 'It's like everything else over here – they don't know what they're at.'

This became the theme for the rest of the journey, Gus pointing at everything, even a car with a flat tyre, and saying in a told-you-so voice, 'Look at that for God's sake – some country.' For a while I entered in, sharing his impulse to see things fail. But it went so out of control that I became uneasy and began to withdraw when I sensed that we were working our way through a litany of failures, leaving just enough time in between each one for the unspoken response; I'm glad I don't have to live here – or, I'm glad I left this godforsaken place.

But I don't think it would have made much difference whether I continued to take part in that litany or not because I knew from other visits down the years that no matter what I did a sense of loss would creep up anyway and seize me in a hold from which I could not release myself.

When we turned off the main road and entered a landscape that was familiar I found myself resisting the first trickle of memories, aware that it could become an overwhelming flood. As we drove past Dineen's I tried to catch a glimpse of the house, forgetting that it was not possible to see it from the road. I was already drifting back to the opening night of the carnival when Gus announced that the hearse was slowing down.

Up ahead three figures were flagging it down. A minute or two later I saw Queenie, Devoy and Maguire. I reckoned they had met at the station where Queenie, as planned, had come to meet us off the afternoon train. Once they had sorted out what was going on they must have decided to walk out to meet the hearse.

When we got out of the car Queenie, with her hand clasping her lower back, was telling the hearse driver that she thought her hip was going to dislocate. This quickly became the issue of the moment, with everyone fretting and fussing over Queenie, making it all look like the scene of a road accident.

Devoy supported her on one side and I supported her on the other while she eased herself into the passenger seat, the only place, she kept telling us, where she had enough leg room to make sure she did not put her hip out. While we were doing this – and it took at least ten minutes – I saw Maguire taking an Irish flag from the large Marks and Spencer bag he had carried since we got on the train at Euston. Distracted by the job of getting Queenie into the car, it did not occur to me what he was going to do with it, right up to the moment when the hearse driver opened the hatch door and Maguire spread the flag over my father's coffin. I was pleased. I think we all were, not so much that the flag had been draped over the coffin but that my father's funeral had become the main focus of the day again.

I walked behind the hearse with Devoy and Maguire, talking a little at first but then stopping altogether as we entered the town. They kept falling behind and each time I slowed down until they caught up. Eventually Devoy made it clear that I should walk directly behind the coffin, with them following a few steps behind me. It was at that point, ahead, somehow in charge of my father's return home, that I felt a wave of sadness. I imagined for a moment that I would not be able to continue walking. Only when that sadness fused with the anger I still felt, did I know I would be able to continue. By the time I did take the next step forward I was fully in the grip of that anger, struggling to contain an urge to shout at the small groups of people who stopped to have a look. But it did not come to that, or anywhere near it, because

I knew that nothing I could say would change the way they stared or the way they nodded to each other before they said: home from England.

As we approached Dineen's office the big navy blue blind was pulled down. It was the first sign that we belonged. I wanted to rush over and say thanks. I wanted to make something of it, let the people standing gawking at us know who we were and who my father was. But in that same moment I wanted it all to be over. I wanted to be back in London, living a life that, there and then on Main Street, seemed full of possibilities. I began to savour the thought of returning.

Someone gripped my arm just above the elbow. A voice whispered, 'Himself is away, but he rang the office a while ago and I told him the news. He said to convey his deepest sympathy and he'll definitely be here for the burial in the morning.'

I turned and there, large as life, was Hegarty. I was so glad to see him that I did not even try to make sense of what he said.

He walked beside me to the end of the town, striding along, full of himself in the way he always was. And I kept pace, very relieved to be reinstated and saved from the humiliation of walking through the town, laying claim to something the people did not seem to realize was rightfully ours. Hegarty spoke once or twice but I did not reply, afraid my voice would break and so betray how close I was to tears.

'I have to go back to the office. If you want to, if you felt like it, you could come over tonight after the removal.'

I managed to say thanks.

After his last visit back, my father told us that Hegarty was working with Dineen as an apprentice auctioneer and so I knew where he was going when he said 'the office'. What I didn't know, and what Queenie was very anxious to tell me, was that Hegarty's job in Dineen's office was quickly followed by Hegarty's marriage to Dineen's youngest daughter, Valerie.

And Queenie, releasing bits of the story in a way she considered tactful, added, 'You'll see the rest for yourself, when you go over after the removal.'

More people than I expected turned up at the church that evening and Bríd, despite how drawn and ravaged she looked, was pleased and at one stage visibly delighted when a woman I did not know walked up to shake hands and stood chatting for a few minutes.

'There'll be an even bigger crowd here in the morning,' Hegarty said as he led the way towards a gleaming silver Merc.

'I needn't tell you who owns this. He's on his way back from his holidays so this is the last of it I'll have.' But his tone, until then full of resignation, turned to glee. 'He goes three times a year. Tenerife – for his arthritis.'

I expected Hegarty to tear along but he was cautious, creeping through the town and slowing down to about five miles an hour as we drove up the avenue to the big house.

'We're on this side,' he said, pointing to what looked like a long line of outbuildings. But it turned out to be one side of an enclosed yard which could only be entered through an arch at the opposite side. Inside, to the right of the arch there was a double door with a line of yellow light filtering out onto the cobbled stones.

Hegarty walked right in and straight through into the room beyond, pushing the door closed behind him. I stood looking at a girl I did not recognize but knew must be Valerie Dineen. She smiled at me as she turned the tiny baby she was holding around, placing it gently on her shoulder and holding it there with one hand. She then walked forward with her other hand held out.

'Valerie Dineen. I can't get used to calling myself Valerie Hegarty – not to mention Mrs Hegarty. That's what the butcher started calling me the first morning I went in after we got back from our honeymoon. And there was me, looking around the shop, not knowing who he was talking to. And this is Baby Al,' she said, turning so as I could see the baby's face.

'Alan Hegarty,' I said, smiling at the tiny creased face, burrowing into his mother's neck.

'No actually, not Alan – Alphonsus, after Daddy. Not that he was over the moon about it all. To be honest with you, he was raging. But Mammy was great. Wasn't she?' she said to Hegarty who strolled back into the room wearing different clothes, an emerald green V-necked jumper and beige trousers.

He nodded.

'You're a teacher in London, aren't you?'

'Yes.' I wanted to say more but I couldn't think of anything, so I just said 'Yes' again, and awkwardly added, 'in London.'

'I don't know how you can stand looking at the punks with those razor blades and pins.'

'You get used to it.'

'Well I didn't. They frightened the life out of me – and I was there for nearly six weeks last year.'

'On holiday?'

'No, sort of business really. A course. Interior design. I came home at the weekends. It started out with Daddy wanting the drawing-room and dining-room restored to what they looked like when he worked here a million years ago.'

She lifted the baby off her shoulder and holding it out directly in front of her, continued to talk, addressing everything to it.

'He got an interior decorator, an interior decorator, didn't he? All the way down from Dublin. An interior decorator. But the quote-sie-wote-sie for the job sent him into a rage. Didn't it? isn't that what it did – Alsie Palsie? Sent Grandaddy into one of his rages.'

Then glancing at me and lowering her voice to a confidential whisper, as if she did not want the baby to hear, she said, 'To calm Daddy down Mammy said that me and her would be able to do it for half the price. I didn't have much on my hands at the time. Not like now. Isn't that right – a full time job you are, aren't you?' The baby yawned. 'He's not tired, you know, he's only just after getting up. Anyway, I didn't have a clue what the place looked like, everything – and I mean everything – was burned in the fire all those years ago. To cut a long story short,' at this point Hegarty raised his eyes upwards, 'I tracked down some relations of the Forestocks, looking for photographs or something about the place showing what it was like. And sure enough . . .'

Nodding in my direction Hegarty said, 'Look, we're going to slip out for an hour or so.'

'They live in Hampstead. Do you know it?'

'Yes,' I replied, 'I know it well,' and I tried to indicate that I could not say more by looking intently at Hegarty, standing at the door jingling the car keys.

'And then I had to get the wallpaper – silk embossed. And the material – hand-printed. It all ended up costing twice as much, but Mammy made sure that Daddy was none the wiser.'

'We won't be long,' Hegarty said as he gestured to me to follow him out into the courtyard.

'Fine, but remember you're better off not going anywhere too local. Daddy says people won't bring their business to you if you're rubbing shoulders with them every day, maybe you should go into the new golf club in Kilkenny.'

Then from the doorway she said, 'Did he tell you that Daddy rang from the airport and when he heard the news he sent his deepest sympathy. He'll be here in time for the Mass and burial in the morning.'

As we drove away she was smiling and waving, peculiarly happy in herself.

When we got into the golf club bar, some people Hegarty knew called him over to where they were sitting. We spent the next couple of hours with them, most of the time listening to stories about a bank manager who had been in the town in the fifties. 'A bit of a character,' one of them confided to me at the end of each of these stories.

Hegarty dropped me back at Queenie's about midnight and said that if I felt like it we could go for a few drinks the following night as well. Then, pushing himself back against the seat until his arms were in a straight line from his shoulders to the steering wheel, said, 'I needn't tell you that if we go, it won't be in this luxury we'll be going.'

When I got in there was a note on the table, in Queenie's big babyish handwriting, telling me that I was to sleep on the couch. I put the couch cushions on the ground, added the cushions from the chair and was asleep within minutes.

The next morning, Gus was busy organizing everyone. Bríd, he announced would sit in the front passenger seat of the funeral car, while Agnes, Queenie, Lil and myself would sit in the back. As he spoke he went through the movements of people getting into a car, drawing imaginary divisions between them and then standing back to look at the arrangement. But just as we were all about to leave, Queenie, linking arms with Bríd, turned around and in a voice full of authority said to Gus, 'My sister and I will be walking down to the church. Walking.' He went to speak but Queenie made it very clear that she had not finished, 'Walking, as we always have done and always will do.'

As I watched them walk out the gate, arm in arm, I knew they would ultimately end their days together in that much talked about luxurious extension. And then I found myself thinking about the way we used to go to Queenie's house every Sunday morning and walk down to the church with her and Michael. In a way, things had not changed very much. Queenie was in charge again just as she had been on those Sunday mornings. After days of uncertainty, floundering around on unfamiliar terrain, the police station, the morgue and then the undertakers, I was relieved to be in a world more enduring than any of the events taking place in it.

A small group stood outside the church, Devoy, Maguire, Dineen and Hegarty. As we approached I saw Hegarty nudge Dineen and then walk quickly into the church. I expected Dineen to go in too, but he waited outside and when we were a few yards away, walked forward with his hand stretched out and his tanned face full of sympathy. Bríd stumbled towards him and remained in the firm clutch of his handshake for several minutes. Queenie looked on like a patient chaperone, ignoring Maguire and Devoy who had edged their way over to her, trying to tell her that the flag had been removed from the coffin.

Dineen, aware of what was going on, turned to Queenie and said, 'He was a great man. There's no doubt about that. But you know and I know and the Lord knows that in the present situation that flag is an insult on a coffin.'

'The Irish flag,' Maguire said, pausing between every word and waving his finger at Dineen, 'never was and never will be an insult to a man that was loyal to his country until the day he died – and in his time did his bit for the cause.'

'Now,' Dineen said in a low, devout voice, 'this isn't the time for politics, not here in front of the church with the widow waiting to go into her husband's Requiem Mass.'

With that, he ushered Bríd into the church, standing back with exaggerated gallantry, while she and Queenie made their way up to the front pew.

I learned later that that exchange between Dineen and Maguire was the last volley of shots in a full-scale row that had been going on outside the church for some time before we got there. Dineen and Hegarty had arrived early, strode in, walked straight up to the coffin, removed the flag and replaced it with an enormous arrangement of flowers. When Maguire and Devoy arrived, someone in the church told them what had happened and they went out to where Dineen and Hegarty were waiting for us. The row that followed was reported by several people who heard it on their way in. By all accounts, Hegarty was relentless in his defence of his father-in-law and himself 'against the two Englishmen'.

After the burial, when we were all standing about outside the graveyard, Bríd asked me to go over and thank Dineen for the flowers. She told me she had already done so, but added, 'They are so beautiful, we should all make it our business to say thanks.' Dineen was talking to a small group of people who were beginning to disperse, so I stood at a little distance from him and waited.

'A harmless poor ould divil,' he said, nodding his head. As they walked away the people nodded in agreement. 'A harmless poor ould divil,' Dineen said again and then, heading for his car, added, 'God rest his soul.'

I backed away, anxious that he would not turn around and see that I had overheard him. I was hurt to the quick. But so much fell into place so quickly that a desire for vengeance replaced the hurt I felt. I had glimpsed what seemed like my father's life and in that instant I wanted to say something about it to Dineen and the others. At the same time I knew very well that nothing I could say to them would stop them from summing up that life in the way they had. 'A harmless poor ould divil, home from England, God rest his soul.'

*

I thought that the need I felt to tell people about him would go away once I was back in London. But it did not. If anything, I became more determined – continually haunted by the threadbare epitaph given by people he always considered his own.

Without a definite plan, I began gathering facts about him, spurred by the belief that there had been a great deal more to his life than those people knew. I imagined, while I was gathering those facts, that the more details about his life I unearthed the more effectively I could piece it together. There was no difficulty in getting facts – born in 1907, he was the only child of his father's second marriage. Five stepbrothers emigrated before he was born or when he was very young. Started work as a farm labourer when he left school in 1921. Seasonal work, thinning beet, sowing potatoes, that sort of thing. Cycled to hurling matches the length and breadth of the country. Lived with his mother, a semi-invalid for most of her later years. A year after she died – to the day – he married Bríd. He was forty. Queenie said he had proposed to her ten years earlier. His mother, her mother, the war. Money.

After months of mulling over these and a host of other facts the picture was not getting any more distinct. I had all but given up when it began to dawn on me that I could not hope to tell his story without telling my own. Reaching that point was a little like climbing to the top of a very high ridge: a vantage point from which I could see my fields becoming his fields. In the far distance, beyond those fields, his war for independence began to look like one of the war games we played during those hot August days when our stories first began to merge.